Fiston

A Tale of Two Moggies

Fiston

A Tale of Two Moggies

Harold Jacobs

The Pentland Press Limited
Edinburgh • Cambridge • Durham • USA

First published in 1996 by
The Pentland Press Ltd.
1 Hutton Close
South Church
Bishop Auckland
Durham

British Library Cataloguing in Publication Data.
A Catalogue record for this book is available
from the British Library.

ISBN 1 85821 436 X

Typeset by CBS, Felixstowe, Suffolk
Printed and bound by Antony Rowe Ltd., Chippenham

To: Our Pets,
to whom we owe so much.

Foreword

During and after Harold Jacobs' first days as a neurologist he loved to create laughter. He has long been widely admired by many friends in Africa, Canada and the United Kingdom as an unpaid professional humorist. His early, hilarious piece, the classic *Cats* was published by the Canadian Medical Journal. Recently, the author has devoted more time to writing and has completed two novels.

With his droll tale of *Fiston* he returns to his early love of cats. His animals evoke our feelings and delight with their curious displays of personality and emotion. We find not too heavily human, or inhuman traits in the main characters. Rather, readers will find some glorious spoofs on mankind's own humour and institutions.

There are varieties on the theme. Immaturity will sometimes appear in cases of sweet intentions but, also, of extreme selfishness. The theme has been a traditional subject for laughmongers. Harold Jacobs likes to apply such a joking, frustration-revealing approach to his animals. One lady cat hopes she may fall deeply enough in love with a sorry eunuch to make a sexless match attractive. But the would-be hero's regular bouts of infantile hedonism would not allow even excellent sex to preserve a long romantic relationship. The author draws on his extended knowledge of friends, colleagues, patients and relatives to illuminate his own realm of cats and dogs, as well as human tragicomedy. The result is very funny.

Fiston also throws much needed light, through a writer's example, on the often misunderstood issues about what is called pornography. Writers have good taste – or they do not. It is the taste, not the topic, which divides the gracious and amusing from purveyors of mere dirt. Harold Jacobs quite wisely allows his animals to be mature enough to philosophize, at times, about mating, dating and defecating. And here is another good reason for recommending Fiston to children and adults alike.

Jane Austen's cattiest conversation, like beasts' talk in *Aesop's Fables* and George Orwell's *Animal Farm*, seem to have found a worthy successor.

John King Farlow.

Chapter 1

The Trial

'Well,' murmured the suave, shorthaired, grey cat, as he surveyed his pads, pink protruding islands amidst the furry bushes of his elegant paws, 'where shall I begin? Let's see . . . it all started seven years ago. I have,' he paused several seconds for effect, 'been haunted by certain events in my childhood – you might well ask who hasn't? – but bear with me. I must set the stage. Seven years ago I was just a measly, six months old, abused kitten, an orphan, but one who eventually found asylum in the animal shelter.'

The learned judge, blinking furiously, scribbled on a note pad.

The learned grey wigged counsels for the prosecution and the defence, sitting at separate desks, yawned and fiddled with their respective briefs.

'From there, the animal shelter, I was adopted by a human family that consisted of one,' he sniffed derisively, 'ineffectual male, a dominant female, and twin surly, egocentric young female offspring. They spent *every* morning reading a column by a newspaper sage called Ann Landers, and lounging around depositing clothes and dirty dishes for me to lick up. All lived together in a fashionable, "post modern" luxury house. To me it looked just like a collection of large, faceless white blocks. Actually,' he paused, lost in thought, 'I should say that before my sojourn in the animal shelter I had, albeit briefly, enjoyed a bit of a wild, free, adolescence. Unfortunately, I was adopted by a first "owner" during that period, another miserable example of the human race. He'd taken, if I may say so, an inexplicably jaundiced view of an ancient routine male tom-cats have. I refer to spraying out territory in our neighbourhood with an irresistible aroma.'

The judge looked up, tapped his lips with a furry paw, and nodded empathetically. He started to blink rapidly and scribbled away on his pad.

'Spreading pheromones, I believe, is the current scientific description,' said his Lordship, helpfully.

'I had no idea *my* owner would take such offence. But, of course, he was from an ignorant, domineering species . . . a human! They prefer to live in their own obnoxious environment. Artificial perfumes! Weird scents with weird names! Nothing . . . nothing natural! Do you know that humans submerge their bodies in water! Imagine it! Those twins use enough water to slake the thirst of a herd of elephant in the dry season on the plains of Africa. What a waste of lovely water. And it does nothing for their temperament. And the amount of soap! Some of them are known to wash . . . all over . . . with tons of smelly soap!' The grey cat's sneer softened into a wistful expression, and he let out a long, one of many, soft sighs. 'They do feed me when they remember, so they can't be all bad . . . but I digress.'

The prosecuting counsel rose to his hind legs.

'What is it?' snapped his Lordship. 'Whatever it is . . . it's overruled.'

The prosecutor pursed his lips, gave a slight bow, and sat

down.

'On the other hand,' the grey cat, unruffled by the brief exchange, glanced at the judge. He continued, 'We are a green species . . . natural . . . nothing phony about us. Ours is . . . ahh . . . such a wondrous pong, er, aroma,' Fiston, the grey tom, paused to blink away a tiny tear as the audience stirred, 'I do miss that part of my existence . . . but never mind. We have to accept our fate. The part of my life that is forever lost,' he shrugged mournfully.

'Please . . . let me continue,' he added hastily, just as the judge began to open his mouth, 'this is what really happened. I'll be as short as possible. I was whipped off to the local vet, supposedly a cat fancier – he kissed me on the nose to prove it – and willy-nilly, without *any* consent on my part, money changed hands, and my privates were history, quick as a wink. No tears for my forfeited heirs. When I got over the shock of the operation, I was overcome with a deep depression. And later, when it really sank in, I became suicidal. I moped and wept and wept like mad. I refused to eat. (From personal observation I am familiar with this behaviour in young, hysterical, human females).'

At that moment a beautiful cat in exquisitely groomed white fur, leaned forward and signalled urgently to Fiston curled up in the witness box. Fiston distracted, paused in mid sentence, his eyes opened wide. From the well of the court he saw her pass a note to Boris, his bewigged defence lawyer. What was this? He squinted, rubbed his eyes, turned to stare at his lawyer now peering at the note. But when Fiston looked up she'd left the court. The lawyer continued to study the note. Fiston, puzzled, resumed his tale.

'For weeks I lay curled up in my basket, refusing food and

drink. I wept many a silent tear. *No one noticed*. After a month, when my mental wounds had healed, I decided I'd had enough of this way of life. I'd jolly well show them it didn't matter, not for nothing was I known as *The Great Grey One* . . . a Russian Blue through and through. You see I was psyching myself up. Little did I guess what humiliation lay in store!'

The judge looked up from his desk, stared earnestly at the dramatic witness, then resumed writing. The prosecutor shook his head and raised his eyes to the ceiling.

'One day, two weeks later, a Siamese feline from next door, literally oozing romance strolled into my territory. I moved over to welcome and inspect her. I gave her my usual cool, dispassionate stare and greeted her – as I knew she'd expected – without thinking twice.

'Ooooh, miaaooowww,' I heard her moan expectantly. 'Oh, oooh, Fiston!'

'I yawned, I pretended to be ever so blasé about the whole business. But then, when it was all set . . . bloody horrors . . . I, my body, failed! Nothing happened. I tried and tried, my humiliation growing. In desperation I opened my mouth and roared like a lion. (I'd seen them do that on TV), but to no avail . . . in the end, mortified, I slunk off. This was too much.' Fiston shook his head and bared his fangs, 'I vowed to get even with those humans responsible for my failure.'

The prosecutor looked blankly at the accused, trying to size him up. For the second time in a few minutes he shook his furry head thoughtfully. What a card!

'And thus, m'lord,' the grey cat addressed the learned Judge, 'I – normally a reasonable cat person – with my mind overheated, laid plans for revenge. In this case, on any or all humans, and not only on those who had maltreated me. But, more than anything, I chose those *particular* humans who happened to be housing me at present.

'You see,' he went on, inspecting his tail end and neighbouring parts carefully, 'I was confused as well as terribly depressed! I wanted to help myself . . . to survive, and get even. Wasn't it that so-called great American man, one Joseph Kennedy, who said, "Don't get mad, get even"?' Fiston turned to face the silent jury and added, softly, 'I chose my targets for two reasons.'

'Yes, yes,' encouraged the enthralled judge. This was better than watching movies.

'The plain fact is I was persistently harassed, subjected to acute embarrassments – the result of *constant* smothering and the ridiculous, patronizing, nauseating baby talk from those two immature twin females. It weighed on my mind to the extent that I thought there seemed to be no escape! No evading their overbearing, cloying presence. I had no privacy. Nowhere to go. No space. I had to flee!'

Fiston, eyes hooded, slowly surveyed the packed courtroom.

'Furthermore, there is the matter of my lost virility. As you well know, m'lord, tom-cats are the last bastion of independent masculinity. But how did I fit in now?' he asked, rhetorically, 'I'm trapped! Emasculated! *Humans* are entirely responsible for my sad, lost plight. Oh dear,' he sighed, gazing at the ceiling, 'instead of understanding, for what seemed like *endless* hours, those bloody teenagers caressed me near my private fur, totally ignoring or understanding me. I didn't want to be a stuffed toy. *I pretended* I liked it, but inside me there was nothing, no emotion, only disgust. It was a sham . . . a mechanical . . . act. If I so much as purred those silly girls went wild. It was sickening. What little insight adolescent humans have,' he shook his head, 'and what little maturity at that age, and later, if my memory

5

serves me right.

'In the end, in despair, I began to exploit their weaknesses. I tantalized them with gifts. I caught and delivered . . . several lesser creatures. You know, lizards, magpies, frogs, the sort our mothers used to use as 'trainers' when we were kittens. I'd bring them to the house, partly decomposed. Eeoughh,' Fiston pulled a face, 'how I detested those livers and gall bladders. But I noticed, by their reactions, that I was inviolate. No one reproached me. *I could do no wrong.* The young specimens of the human species invariably responded to my offerings by making cooing and oooing noises – I believe that's what they call those human sounds – with delight!

'"Look Mummy," I heard them cry, "the darling boy's brought up a present. Isn't he too cute? He wants us to share." Share? And then, before I could escape, they'd smother me with more slobbery kisses and cuddles. That's what they call those disgusting human activities. One young chronically angry female actually *apologized* to her mother on my behalf! I heard her say something about, "Don't be so negative, mother. Baby robins and squirrels are meant to feed Fiston". The irony is I was trying to shock them. I had more than enough food. I was demonstrating that I killed because it was ingrained in me, a male cat. I was misunderstood! On the other hand it dawned on me that I had them in my power. *I could do no wrong.* I could manipulate them, *at will*.'

The prosecutor rose to his hind legs, his forepaws extended in a wide gesture of exasperation,

'If I may interrupt, m'lord. This imaginative narrative, fascinating though it might be on a stage, has *nothing* to do with the alleged offence.'

The judge, stirred, gathered his wits, and turned to glower at the learned counsel,

'That's for me to decide. Objection overruled.'

Fiston, sizing up the judge, produced another diminutive tear that trickled down his fur covered face, then slithered onto his coal black nose. The room was silent. After a pause, he murmured, plaintively,

'May I continue, sir?'

'Of course,' smiled the judge, baring his even more striking set of yellow fangs.

'Things got worse and worse. At about that time they, dragging me along, moved house. The dominant female wanted more space. She didn't like the teak furniture. The problem was they didn't bother to consult me. After we'd moved, and I'd reconnoitred the land, I had to fight like mad to claim my territory. What a nuisance! It took me several wasted weeks to subdue the neighbourhood felines. A short, violent scrap or two, and the air was cleared. But actually, although I didn't realize it, I was past it . . . my prime, and didn't enjoy fighting at all.' He eyed the chronically somnolent judge, a large Persian cat-type, 'There was one porky Ginger Tom. Quite a problem, he was. But I fixed him,' the grey cat grinned sardonically, 'by feigning an injury. A few complaints from my mesmerized owners to the other owner, and, bingo! there followed a visit for the unsuspecting Ginger Tom to an ever obliging vet. And all was well in my new domain. Poor sap. He had undergone the standard treatment. He'd lost his manhood. (With a bit of cash vets can be persuaded to do this ad lib). I became more and more impressed by my ability to control . . . by my power over the female mind. And I'd manipulated the Ginger Tom to establish my domain over the whole neighbourhood. From then on Ginger, and others, kept out of my way.'

The audience of battered tabbies, ragged alley cats, strays, and elderly blue-black, longhaired females arrayed in the back row of the court, gazed in awed silence. Unfortunately the silence disturbed his Lordship's somnolence. He woke, stirred, and glanced around. The room was deathly quiet. The defending lawyer, in teetering white wig, was standing, poised expectantly before the grey cat in the witness box. The judge's purring faded. Had he missed something exciting? Or simply a point of law?

The prosecutor sat staring into space, his chin cupped in his paws. The performance of the accused, that nonchalant Russian Blue, was nauseatingly effective. For someone, thought the lawyer, faced with a possible death sentence, Fiston was remarkably self-possessed.

'So . . . your altered state of mind was the result of . . . geographical, psychological . . . metaphysical . . . sociological factors? A victim of human maltreatment?' prompted the defending lawyer, while nodding encouragement. 'You were, er, provoked beyond endurance?'

The prosecutor sprang to life.

'Objection . . .'

'Objection overruled,' snapped the judge.

The grey cat nodded and smiled, slightly,

'Absolutely. I was driven . . . you see . . . I wasn't in control of my mind, or my will, if you like. All the emotional battering I'd undergone snapped my sanity. Something had taken over my brain, my *mind. I had no free will.* I had become consumed with an overwhelming primeval lust for revenge against all humans.'

'All inflamed by the disgrace of your er, situation, *and* the humiliation of being constantly manhandled!' added the counsel, helpfully.

'Objection m'lord!' The prosecutor was furiously on his paws again, 'He's being led. There is no evidence that cats have a free will, let alone a "mind". I intend to call an expert witness in this matter, a feline neuro-psychologist, a philosopher of great eminence, who'll expound on this issue. This is preposterous. A preposterous claim. My learned friend is encouraging his witness to fantasize.'

'If it pleases m'lord,' interjected Felix, 'I was merely allowing the accused to have his day in court. If he thinks he's got a mind and a free will, then that's his belief and his privilege. Strange as it may seem my learned friend is himself displaying some sort of mind. Why are we here, if we have no mind?' He paused, '*Res ipsa loquitur*,' he added, with a smile of triumph.

'Objection overruled,' grumbled the judge. All this was becoming too abstruse. 'I agree that the objection is frivolous. I have a mind. Pray continue, Mr Fiston.' The judge slumped back and drifted off into another, deeper stupor. Almost immediately the vision of a smoked haddock danced before him, all in technicolor. He sank steadily into stage four dreaming.

'That was a clever ploy,' whispered an awe-struck junior to Felix, the canny defending lawyer.

'Where was I?' Fiston leaned back to lick the fur of his long, twitching tail and, reflecting, began anew.

'Ah, yes . . . I was talking about my desire for justice. May I continue?' he glanced at the row of lawyers packed around him.

'By all means,' said somebody.

'For the next few months I decided to lie low, except for an occasional caterwaul and foray into the territory claimed by the house dog, Oscar. By the way,' he chuckled to the audience, 'I fixed him too, all right. But that's another story.' Fiston flashed a charming smile, '"The girls", as I believe the female humans in the house were known, grew more and more obsessively infatuated with me. As a direct result my morale deteriorated. They dressed me in all sorts of degrading outfits. I was mortified, but I kept my cool. I did nothing that might annoy their childish minds. In exchange I was allowed to roam and sleep where I pleased. All along I knew my time would come. Plans were hatching.'

'M'lord,' Boris the prosecutor was on his hind paws again, 'this is all very well, but what has this to do with the matter in hand, the act of which this cat stands accused. We seem to be wandering all over the place.'

The defending lawyer arched his back and rose slowly,

'The point is, if your Lordship will bear with me, my client is setting the scene, the background, which led up to the alleged act. Evidence for the said act, I would like to emphasize, is based on circumstantial evidence.'

'Yes, yes,' snapped the judge testily, raising an eyelid, 'don't teach me the law. We are aware of what is going on. Get on with it. Lunch will soon be here.' The judge smacked his chops, curled his whiskers, and lapsed into yet another preprandial, comatose state, and dreamed of myriads of succulent mice scurrying past his nose.

'Please continue,' encouraged the defending barrister. Fiston, ever the cool cat, paused deliberately for several seconds while glancing around the courtroom. His yellow, vertically slit pupils swept over a striking black female in the front row of the public gallery. 'Later,' he mouthed in her direction, 'later.'

'Ever since that operation, I've suffered countless identity crises,' said Fiston, with every appearance of veracity. 'One after another. I don't know who, or what, I am. I'm confused. At times I think I'm going mad . . .'

Fiston realized he'd struck the right chord, the right theme, and paused again to let this sink in. 'All the human mothering made it worse, my confusion I mean. It made me feel so, so . . . well . . . *useless*, you know. Maybe I *was* . . . temporarily . . . looney . . . mad?'

The prosecutor let out a soft derisive laugh. This is too much, he thought, what a ham.

Fiston, enthusiastically developing his new role, fidgeted restlessly. He felt himself tingle all over, under his blue-grey fur. 'I . . . was becoming a sort of half female . . . not a proper, full tom,' his voice trailed to a whisper, 'I thought I might be becoming an hermaphrodite!'

In the stunned silence that followed he played his trump card, 'I became so distraught that *I found myself in an unreal world.* I was *Alice in Wonderland.* Nothing around me was authentic! I was in a total daze. Yet events were taking place around me. I could not direct them. I knew they were not real!

'I found myself compelled to take action! Then I remembered my secret weapon. I thought, this is my last resort, my atomic bomb. It'd be no use letting it off in a desert? What good, I asked myself, is a piece of crap, er, beautiful excreta . . . sorry about the oxymoron . . . in a litter box?'

'Ahhh,' murmured the prosecutor, 'now, at last, we're getting to crux of the matter. At last.'

'No,' said Fiston, 'it *had* to be felt and *smelled, as well as to be visible.* You see? To make my point . . .'

The court room was deathly still. You could've heard a mouse's dropping drop.

'Pray continue,' breathed the defending lawyer.

'One fine day, the opportunity presented. The parents of the twins – who'd never ceased fussing over me – decided to go off and spend some of their filthy lucre. They had plenty. The soft, complacent male, who looked like a sleazeball, had already managed to tread on one of my offerings, and was more ill-disposed towards me than ever. Need I say more? I was not in good standing with the elders, only the juniors, of the "club". So I was doubly pleased to see them off the premises.'

'Are we to believe you are pleading extenuating circumstances?' sneered the prosecutor, softly, hardly rising from his seat.

The judge-cat dozed on steadily.

'What d'you think I've been trying to say all along, sir,' purred the grey cat, with barely concealed sarcasm. 'Why am I here? Listen . . . then you'll grasp the facts, and understand my predicament.'

At this the judge woke, harrumphed, sat up, raised a lip, displaying yellow, sardine stained, incisors.

'I must warn you, Mr Fiston. Any more of that and I'll cite you for contempt.'

In a flash the defending counsel was back on his hind paws, 'I apologize for my client. I beg you, sir, to overlook his lapse. Fiston's under tremendous strain. His case has caused a stir throughout the feline world. All eyes are focused on this trial. We may be making history. Even the human's Animals' Rights Activists and TV cameras are in court. We,' he glanced over his shoulder to an obese, matronly cat with leathery, wrinkled fur, with tufts of short, blonde-red colouring, 'have a society reporter present.'

'TV cameras? Here? First I heard of it,' grumbled the judge.

'Yes, m'lord. It seems this case has excited feminists. Why? I'm not sure why.'

'Perhaps because they see themselves as victims of feline *and* human society?' The judge, preening himself looked around the packed court for approval.

'Trust the crafty bugger to wake up when there's maximum publicity around,' murmured the prosecutor to his junior, 'TV indeed. It's that female reporter. She's usually at horse races. A horsy cat. Can't abide her. Jo-Anne Lumpkin's her moniker. She's all show. Thinks she's one of the beautiful people. Her best friends are horses. Ha!' he laughed, 'Ha! Old Felix tipped her off. She also works part-time in stables, catching mice for a fee. She's no reporter.'

'I see,' said the junior, baffled, 'how do you know all this?'

'Her ex was a buddy of mine. She was invited here by our friend Felix. It's his idea of playing to the gallery ever since he saw "Rumpole and the Strays". Now the judge's onto it too. Let me tell you not so long ago Felix was lounging around those very stables, looking for scraps. Look at him now. Overfed and cocky. Just like that criminal cat on the stand . . .,' his voice trailed away as the learned judge glared in his direction.

'What *are* you meowing about, Boris? Anything we should know?'

'Checking a point of law with my junior counsel, m'lord.'

The dreamy judge nodded to Fiston, the grey cat,

'Pray continue.'

Fiston, not one to miss a chance to show off, ceased licking the area of his private parts, and lowered a back leg, ever so gracefully,

'I laid my plans carefully. I waited until my guardians, the teenybopper humans, were out buying jeans, those strange coverings they wear instead of fur. I crept up the stairs. Ahhh! This was forbidden territory. It had been ingrained in me that

13

I was never allowed in there, the main bedroom. I paused to look around. I didn't fancy a spray of water in the face. I waited with bated breath . . .'

The courtroom was absolutely still.

'A sudden noise in the garden shook me. But it was only Oscar, barking at a magpie. I get terrible headaches from his confounded barking.' Yet another tear glistened on his slitted green irises. On cue the back row of elderly cats dabbed Kleenexes to their moist nostrils. All purring had ceased. There was total, deathly silence.

'I leaped, gracefully, as is my habit, onto the clean duvet, and turned my posterior to face,' he sniggered, 'the pillows. Just to test the air I let out a soft, delicate peté.' Although uncertain about this word, the enraptured audience gasped.

'When I realized my aim was spot on, I opened all valves and let loose the remains of voles, birds, and mice. My angle of attack was terrific. But my main aim – pardon the pun – was to *punish* them and with significant effect. I was making a *statement*. The problem was I was sure no one would suspect me. Here *I* was in control. I was so careful! Strange to say, at that moment I suffered mixed emotions. Was I simply jealous? Of what? I don't know. My motives were confused. For a moment I was frozen in a moment of introspection.'

'What . . .?' began Felix, the defence lawyer and, thinking the better of it, stopped.

'When I regained my senses, the deed done, I rushed from the room, leaped through the open window, and made for the garage. I pushed the door open, and as casually as possible, strolled out and sat myself in full view in Oscar's territory. Oh, happy day. The sun shone. I was in Heaven on that back porch.

'Later that day the noisy teenyboppers returned bearing parcels and disappeared into their rooms. A few moments later one slipped into the master bedroom to thumb through a naughty book, but was so shortsighted and stuffed up, she didn't notice my deposit. Maybe she had a cold. Just as well for her sake.'

'You mean she didn't smell your foul droppings?' interjected the prosecutor, standing. 'Let's not mince words.'

'Objection, my Lord,' the defence too was standing.

'I . . .' interrupted the prosecutor, 'withdraw that remark. I'll not, at this stage, interfere in his fanciful tale of faecal misadventure. Not for the present, at any rate.'

'Time for lunch, the court will adjourn.' The roly poly, long haired judge, rose creakily to his four feet, arched his back, and waddled off to find the red plastic dish awaiting him in the corner of the judge's dining room.

'All rise,' cried the usher, and winked at the court stenographer. 'Time for a lunch of old, cold fishheads.' Adding, sotto voce to the court reporter, 'Care to join me?'

'Quite a show today. Fiston's got that audience and the jurors eating out of his paws,' complained the prosecutor, over lunch, to his junior. 'But let him carry on. You know the saying, "give him enough brown rope" . . .?' Overcome with this novel proverb, the lawyer sniggered until a prolonged sneezing bout convulsed him. 'Let me tell you, sirra, in the end, justice will prevail, or my name's not Boris.'

In the public cafeteria, set amongst an array of trash cans, customers licked steadily at a selections of discarded open tins.

'My wife gets this stuff for me. Saves us a fortune. It's as good as anything you can get in the Super Garbage Dumps chain. Wonderful cat, my wife. She's given us sixteen litters, you know. What a mother . . .' he sighed as his incisors delicately

15

stripped a straggly chicken wing, 'But, to business. We must get our strategy ready. I'm going for the death sentence.'

His junior gasped.

'You are? Really? That's exceedingly rare these days? Only for *excessive* caterwauling and spraying, surely? But for minor crapping? Isn't it three years maximum?'

'Perhaps. But it was the *place*, the locality, not just the motive, the scene of the crime, my dear boy. The place. Calculated to destroy all goodwill built up over centuries between us and humans. It'd be quite different if we were big cats, like our cousins, the lions and tigers. Unfortunately we're completely dependent on goodwill. To be blunt, *we serve no purpose*, we live on charity. Even those dumb canines can do more. Ours is a purely parasitic existence. Let's face it my friend, we need humans more than they need us. We need a roof over our heads. And we cannot let slimy, good-looking, grey cats, cocky ex-toms, wreck it all. Can we? No, I'm afraid it's the noose for him. Let him waffle on. It'll do him no good in the end.'

The junior remained awestruck. The prosecutor, a determined feline, growled deep in his throat. But both knew he faced the battle of a lifetime. His reputation was at stake. He had to win. He had no illusions. He was up against a crafty opponent. For Boris could see, far away in his future, a judge's robes and wig . . . if he played his kitty cards right. Nothing could get in his way. But Boris the prosecutor was painfully aware that a bitter fight still lay ahead. Felix was no pushover.

'Be upstanding for his Lordship,' intoned the clerk of the court. And all rose, or so it seemed, respectfully. A distant cat flap in a door opened. In strolled the judge, in full regalia, a pendulous, bulging, stomach scraping the courtroom floor. Immediately he curled up heavily in the basket on the bench.

The audience sat. The numerous court officers made themselves comfortable. The gallery was packed to the gills. News of the sensational trial had spread around the neighbourhood. Not a single seat was left empty. It was standing room only. The stench of cat was, almost, too heady. In the distance an unhappy dog barked mournfully. That day there were no cats to be chased . . . anywhere.

The drama continued.

'M'lord,' the prosecutor rose smoothly, 'on a point of order . . .'

'Yes, yes, what is it?' The judge had not yet divested himself of a persistent fur ball and was extremely cantankerous. This was a chronic problem. He'd have to stop his grooming or, worse still, visit the vet! Bloody vets. Made too much money. The judge sighed. His wife was always at him to get his fur professionally trimmed. What a life. And here before him, was that Lothario of a cat enjoying perfect health and, perhaps, freedom. It occurred to him that it might do his, the judge's, reputation a power of good if he invoked the death penalty? Maybe a supreme court appointment lay ahead?

Seemingly unaware of the cloud assembling over him, Fiston ambled to the witness box and curled up, one paw languidly outstretched. Optimistically he basked, with evident pleasure, in the notoriety of the moment.

'You are still under oath,' reminded the Clerk of the Court. Fiston raised his eyebrows and nodded agreeably.

'M'lord,' began Boris the prosecutor, 'I submit that the witness has recounted what amounts to a confession in open court, and that he did the deed of which he stands accused.'

'That's for me and the jury to decide,' growled the judge, coming out of his latest reverie. 'Stick to your job and leave decisions about the law to me. Get on with it.'

'Now . . . sir,' began Felix the defence counsel, adjusting his fur, and addressing Fiston, 'I take you back now to the happenings on that day in October. Can you tell us what transpired next?'

'Ah,' Fiston, by now a celebrity, looked dreamily out of the window. 'Ah, yes. There's not much more really. Some of what I say was repeated to me. Some is personal recollection.'

'Mr Prosecutor,' snapped the judge, waylaying the lawyer, 'any objections?'

'None, m'lord.'

'Not too long after the event,' said Fiston, 'the wife came home and suddenly became all of a dither. In the interval, while they were away, my mind had become icy clear. I inched nearer to the bedroom window to get a hold on what they were up to. I suspected I might be in hot water when I heard them debating. I'd expected a little fuss, some enquiries, but I was taken aback by the speed of events. I was staggered that they apportioned the blame on me. How did they guess? Suddenly I heard my name. I heard phrases like, '"One Life Left". I went cold. I knew that I was in the soup. Furthermore, to my utter horror, I heard them discussing the possibility of taking in a new boarder. My fur froze! What's this? Was I being swapped? I said to myself, only humans could contrive such cruel and unusual punishment!'

'You had no memory of what you'd done?' asked the defence lawyer.

'Not at that time. All I know now is what I'm accused of.'

The judge looked nonplussed,

'But Fiston . . . you've just recounted in considerable detail, what you had done in the bedroom.'

'M'lord, the point is, I'm not sure whether I dreamt it, or whether I was told it, or whether it was a fantasy. I recognize now, as a reasonable cat, that it wasn't a good idea. *If I had been in my right mind I would never have done it.* How could I, with all my feline intelligence, have expected to get away with it?'

Chapter 2

Fiston's Defence

In the distance the city hall clock struck two o'clock. Lunch was over. The main court room under the Palace of Justice, as the decrepit old pub was known, was steadily filling with sated, drowsy, yet fascinated mammals of the feline persuasion. By now news of the trial had aroused universal interest. It was fast becoming a cause célèbre. As a result there was standing room only in the gallery for spectators. Dozens of disappointed onlookers had to be turned away.

'All rise for his Lordship,' yowled the clerk of the court, partially suppressing a fishy burp. The whole court rose to its feet. The hatch leading to the Judge's chambers opened upwards and his Lordship stalked in, visibly heavier, whiskers a'twitch. With a noticeable effort he hoisted himself onto his favourite perch, a red velvet cushion, circled a few times, and settled. He acknowledged the presence of the court with a brief nod. The audience resumed their seats.

'M'lord,' Felix, the defending counsel, came forward and bowed deferentially, 'if it please m'lord, I wish to call an expert witness. I have his curriculum vitae.'

'Very well. Hand it over to the clerk of the court.'

The defence lawyer presented a 50 page sheaf of papers with

an addendum numbered with Roman numerals. In turn the clerk of the court handed it to the judge and to the prosecutor.

'Mark it exhibit "C".'

'I call Doctor Pierre von Straws. Please take the stand, Doctor von Straws,' ordered the clerk of the court, 'take the Bible in your right paw.' Doctor von Straws, a portly tabby with straggly blond whiskers, and a pompous, dignified demeanour, answered the time honoured questions in a firm, London accent. He swore never to lie.

'Please state your name,' began the defence attorney, 'and your profession.'

This opportunity to pronounce seemed to please Doctor von Straws who launched into a prepared statement. Everyone in the court was impressed by his resonant voice, his magnificent delivery, and by his impeccable credentials. It turned out that he was, among other matters, a leading forensic neuro-psychiatrist who'd published a reference work on feline behaviour, now a standard textbook in countries as far away as the Gold Coast of Africa. As a side line he was also an expert in feline sleep disorders. The judge, on hearing about the latter, ruffled his fur coat hastily and raised drooping eyelids. He shook his head vigorously and breathed in deeply, but with little success. An overwhelming torpor reasserted itself, and his eyelids began to droop. Doctor von Straws noting this behaviour pursed his lips and made notes in a tiny black book. Those still waking members of the court were impressed.

'Doctor von Straws,' began the defence lawyer, 'you are acquainted with Fiston, the accused?'

'I am.'

'Have you had occasion to examine him?'

'I have.'

21

'Before I ask you for your opinion, I'd like to ask you an hypothetical question.' Doctor von Straws whose whole existence, professionally speaking, was based on hypotheses and correlations, waited patiently. He had a stock answer ready.

The hypothetical question lasted thirty minutes and the reply, including interruptions, another thirty minutes. By this time his lordship was completely comatose and the prosecutor in a permanent daydream. Doctor von Straws made more notes for his next paper on Drowsiness in the Feline Legal Profession.

'What then, doctor, is your opinion in the case of Fiston?'

The court roused. The judge stirred and, like a narcoleptic, surfaced just in time.

'It's my considered opinion and diagnosis that Fiston, under great duress, was in what we call a "Fugue State".' Doctor von Straws using his forepaws made a sign in the air to suggest double quotes, 'Either that or he was in a state called Total Panic Disarray. Or, failing that, he is still suffering from a Pseudo-False-Memory Syndrome. There are no other possibilities,' uttered the great forensic psychiatrist, with quiet emphasis.

'No more questions,' announced the defence counsel, then changed his mind. 'Would that explain Fiston's actions? Do you mean, are you suggesting, he was not responsible for his actions?'

'Exactly.'

The prosecutor, gathering his bewildered wits, rose to his feet. He shuffled, for what seemed like ages, through his notes. Finally, he looked up and smiled disarmingly at the eminent scientist-doctor.

'Let me get this straight, Doctor von Straws,' he said in the friendliest of tones, 'you know all this, came to these assured

conclusions, without being at the scene of the, er, incidents?'
'Yes.'
'Based only on what the accused, Fiston, told you?'
Dr Straws was ready for this,
'That is correct. I have great experience in such matters.'
'How do you come to your conclusions?'
'I read clues, body language. I go over details again and again.
I deal with the mind. Everything Fiston said made it clear he
was acting out a dream. Lucid dreaming is the phrase. He was
not entirely conscious, he was semi-dreaming, when he was, er,
doing what he did. It is like . . . you've heard of sleep walking,
sleep talking, and sleep violence?'

The court had no clue. But it was too abashed to ask.

The judge responded with his practised judicial glower,
artfully designed to cloak difficult situations. No one guessed
he was in the dark too. No one, he thought, can wade through
this stupid mumbo-jumbo. Bloody psychological quack. And
he smiled sweetly at the great expert witness.

The prosecutor was not about to give up. In true courtroom
style he dropped his easygoing stance, stiffened his back, and
gave every impression of great, but puzzled indignation.

'I'm sorry sir, I don't understand,' he sneered, 'please explain
to the court how you, er, dreamt that up?' and chortled at his
pun. 'What laboratory tests were conducted? For a start, did
you X-ray his head? Did you do an electro-encephalogram?'

'X-ray his head? Encephalogram?' Dr Straws frowned at the
ridiculous suggestions.

'You did no tests?'
'What tests? I need no tests in my work.'
'You made all that up without . . .,'
'Objection . . .,'

'Rephrase that,' grumbled his lordship.

'Let me put it this way, er, how came you to all your conclusions? Really . . . Doctor von Straws, you must explain.'

'I'm sorry about this,' smiled the doctor, graciously, 'I'm sorry you're havin' difficulty,' he drawled, 'but it's a scientific matter, y'know. Don't blame yourself. Science is science.'

'Indeed. And this is a court of law.'

'No need to be aggressive, Boris,' reprimanded the judge. 'Let me remind you Doctor von Straws is an accepted and leading medical expert.'

The prosecutor bowed, 'He should be,' he muttered to his junior, 'he charges a tail and a leg for his fifty page reports.' Aloud he said, 'I take your point sir. But I must ask these questions. I am not all clear about what the doctor claims, or how he arrived at his conclusions. I would like to request an adjournment. I must consult with our experts.'

The judge nodded huffily, rose to his full height of six inches, and without further ado strolled out.

'We must fight fire with fire,' said the prosecutor to his array of underlings. 'Find me another shrink. Any one will do. They *always* disagree. Come to think of it get me Dr Babble, he costs even more than Straws.'

In short order Professor Babble, author of no less than seven textbooks, most of which were out of print, was sworn in. Without hesitation he contradicted everything that Doctor Straws had claimed.

It was by now late on Friday afternoon. The case was adjourned for the weekend.

Monday morning, precisely at 10 a.m. his Lordship re-entered a packed courtroom. Wall-to-wall correspondents filled their allocated seats. The gallery was packed. Once again all rose and settled back for another day of unadulterated entertainment the instant his Lordship cuddled up.

Fiston was recalled. Familiar with procedure he bowed imperceptibly to the court, and ambled slowly and casually toward the witness stand. The judge, his stomach brimming with breakfast goodies, gave him a friendly smile.

'You are still under oath,' intoned the clerk.

'I take you back now to a certain day in September, a month after the alleged incident,' began his lawyer Felix, studying a paper in his paw. 'Did anything unusual occur in the first week of September 1989?'

'Yes . . . there did,' Fiston, the grey cat, spoke firmly, then paused dramatically. He'd been over this part several times with Felix.

'And what was that? What do you recall?'

Fiston took a deep breath and plunged,

'For years, yes, years, before my alleged crime, *nothing* happened in my house which had not been discussed with me.'

'You mean, within your human family?'

'That's what I mean. Imagine my outrage . . . it was a tremendous shock,' Fiston glanced at the somnolent judge, 'when out of the blue, *a young, female feline* stranger arrived. Not only out of the blue, but blue-eyed! I was stunned . . . nonplussed. I immediately perceived her as an invader, an insolent, conceited, adolescent Siamese cat, that suddenly materialized out of nowhere! I mean,' he turned to face the audience, tears glistening on his bright yellow irises, 'what was I to do? I had not been consulted.

'After putting up with years of sickening cuddling . . . was

25

this my reward? What had happened? In an instant I become a second class member of the clan . . . an outcast . . . a pariah! To say I was mortified would be a massive understatement. What *could* I do? I'll tell you what I did.' Fiston paused and gazed in apparent despair at the jury. 'I staggered off to my favourite chair below floors, my mind in turmoil. I had to think . . . I had to think matters over. But just as I left the area I heard mutterings about new quarters for me . . . oh, insult upon injury . . . what were they plotting? All I could hear reverberating in my mind was, "Look at him, poor dear, what a shame, poor Fiston's sulking! He'll get used to her. Won't you, baby?" and "That'll teach him to foul the duvet,"' snarled the non-dominant male.

'Oh God,' Fiston's voice broke, 'how can I explain to you how I felt? Think of my utter dejection at that moment. In this way an hour of misery slowly passed. Then I thought to myself, if I'm to be hanged for an alleged, er, crap, *I might as well go for broke.*'

The judge frowned at the mixed metaphors, but let them pass. He wasn't sure if he'd been caught catnapping.

'It occurred to me that it was inexplicable that no one, not for an *instant*, had blamed Oscar for what'd happened. How did they know it was not him?'

'Oscar?' asked the judge, blinking a bleary eye. 'I don't follow. Why should they have thought about this . . . this . . . Oscar? Who is Oscar?'

'A dog! He lived in the same house. *He never used a litter box.* In fact the garden was almost destroyed by his efforts. An assertive beast of an animal. We all know dogs! And he had free reign, could wander around the house, *including the master bedroom.* Whereas I was not allowed in! It could have been him.

When I regained my equilibrium I decided to lay a smoke screen and to implicate Oscar.'

'You planned all this . . . while you were in a Fugue State?' Boris, an actor in his own right, was a picture of disbelief.

'No, not then. I'm talking about afterwards! I'm referring to the Siamese cat that had been foisted on me and Oscar the horrible dog! I wanted to kill two birds with one, er . . . one stone.'

'You mean . . . one crap?' muttered Boris.

'Whazzat?' demanded the judge, rousing.

'I was clearing my throat, m'lord.'

'I know now it was a mistake,' continued Fiston smoothly, 'but I was desperate. I was counting on,' replied Fiston, wearily, 'the girls assuming my innocence. I had always been innocent in their eyes! Why not now? The only other mammal around at the time of the, er, incident, was Oscar. I thought it would be an easy deduction.'

'Well, it wasn't,' smirked his lordship, 'and weren't you, a short while ago, claiming loss of memory of your misdeed? Now you seem to have been planning to extricate yourself? Kindly explain.'

'Score one for the great judge,' muttered the prosecutor under his breath.

Fiston, paused, licked his chops, and took a deep breath,

'Yes, sir, that's the trouble. I was acting on information, from others, about my alleged actions in the bedroom. By some weird instinct *they guessed it had to be me*. I was fighting for myself. I knew I wasn't guilty, but who would believe me? Do I make myself clear?'

'No,' said the judge.

Fiston, playing for time, paused to wipe watery eyes with a

curled paw.

'Do not distress yourself,' said the judge, softening, and began himself to dab his eyes with a red handkerchief. 'Would you like an adjournment?'

'No thank you, milord,' said Fiston bravely, 'I'll be all right.'

'Bloody ham,' muttered the prosecutor to his junior, 'contradicting himself and trying to weasel out of it. That damn cat should be an actor. I knew a female lawyer once who used those tactics . . . tears flowing in court and all that. Always gets those old lechers, the judges . . . makes them gallant. Talk about phony, unfair tactics. Bah!'

The junior counsel stared curiously at him. What ambitions lay hidden under *his* furry legal skin?

The judge blew delicate, flaring nostrils in a red handkerchief.

'Go on,' urged Felix the defending counsel, in the hushed tones used by lawyers sensing an opportunity. He knew they might be on a winning streak with this excellent, albeit erratic, witness. The extravagant display of emotion impressed the members of the jury – and even the somnolent judge. Fiston held them all in a tight spell. One could have heard a fishbone snap.

'Ah, that awful day. On top of being wrongly accused, another disaster was upon me. Years of happiness, then in an instant . . . sheer misery!' sniffed Fiston, playing his role to the hilt, 'In one blinding instant all was changed. Instead of Oscar howling in the doghouse, in the background I could hear disloyal oohings and cooings, *but not for me!* A new identity had entered the scene . . . a new cat. I found myself with the task of coming face to face with a Siamese! She was already in the house! Where had she come from?

'"Isn't she cute," the treacherous humans bleated. "Look, she jumps sideways, the little darling." What a blow! My only thought was to leave there and then . . . to get out . . . forever. This was no longer my home. I would go off into the wide blue yonder . . . but where? Who would have me? Dimly, sadly, I tried a desperate tactic. I had realized that I had to make a stand. I made a play for attention that always worked. I rotated onto my back, exposed my soft underbelly, and moaned softly. But it didn't work a damn. I heard the girls say, dismissively, "He's having one of his mad days again."

'In the end all I could come up with was a dignified retreat. I couldn't help interjecting a furious hiss as I sailed off. I'm only human, er, feline. I'm not perfect. Who is?'

The judge having recovered his judicial frame of mind, wrote something in his notebook and paused to groom the fur surrounding his derriere.

'What ethnic derivation, did you say, was this new . . . addition?'

'Thai, or in feline language, a Siamese. A recent immigrant,' breathed Fiston in a barely audible whisper. The effect was electric. A sigh starting amongst the ragged strays swept around the room. All purring had ceased as if turned off by a master switch. The judge blinked, sneezed loudly, and made a further note.

'Objection, m'lord,' Boris the prosecutor was on all four feet. 'We are not here to discuss racial origins; we are not here to cast racist slurs. We are all brothers and sisters under the skin. Being Siamese is irrelevant. This is not South Africa!'

'Objection sustained,' intoned his Lordship, who recently promoted from a lower court, was enjoying his judicial powers. He cast a well rehearsed, severe look at Fiston and his defending counsel. 'Keep to the point,' he snapped, 'be so kind as to avoid using my court as a vehicle for your racist views, whatever they are.'

'M'lord,' objected Felix the defending lawyer in contrite tones, 'my client intended no slur. But we cannot escape the fact that the Siamese are beautiful people . . . and opportunists. They derive from a region where life for cats is quite special. They have different values. In Thailand, or Siam, as it was, cats are revered and live in great temples. Life in that part of the world is . . . anointed with sex . . . one hears of gangs . . . drugs . . .'

'Look,' snapped the judge, intrigued despite himself, 'perhaps I have not made myself clear? You are not to take that tack. Do not make political speeches. One more remark like that and I'll cite you for contempt!' The silence that followed his Lordship's outburst in the court was palpable.

Fiston was not dismayed. The grey cat reached for a glass of milk and took a long drink.

'So, in the final analysis, at that moment in time, I had,' he continued, softly and sadly, as the judge dozed off, 'made up my mind to settle an old score with the male human and Oscar, all in one blow. Unfortunately my plans went astray due to circumstances beyond my control. As I said, the family guessed correctly, so we are led to believe. Now I, innocent though I believe I am, had to rehabilitate my image in the eyes of the household. I had to begin, all over again, to re-establish myself. I decided to fight fire with fire and at the same time discredit the Siamese, and somehow, Oscar too. I was not one to give in easily. It's not in my character! Oh, but it was complicated.

'First, I intensified my hunting activities. Day after day I brought home another "trophy" and left it, or its remains, where it *had* to be seen, namely on the front door mat.

'Second, I started an intensified campaign to foul the tortoises' pen, hoping to disparage them. Poor, slow, idiot reptiles carrying their silly houses on their backs! I can tell you the stink in the pen was something to be sniffed to be believed! I thought it only right to expose their random toilet habits.' The grey cat extended his sharp claws, examined them carefully, and allowed himself a derisive smile, 'You see, I was going madder and madder. It was a reversion to my former state when I committed the alleged crime.'

The prosecutor glowered at the grey cat.

'Watch him,' he murmured to his junior, 'and you'll learn. Pay attention. But,' he smiled grimly, 'not to worry, I may have a trick or two up my sleeve. I have my own er, surprises . . . give him enough brown rope, as I said before . . . you know that old adage?'

As if overhearing him, the grey cat moved his slitted, yellow eyes and let them rest on the prosecutor. Their intense, ominous gaze sent a shiver down the junior counsel's long tail. The defending lawyer looked down and studied his notes.

Chapter 3

Carol Intervenes

A sudden commotion in the well of the court attracted the somnolent judge's attention. A glamorous, sheer white queen had risen to her full height.

'Stop!' she cried, imperiously, 'Stop this charade . . . I demand . . . please!' She gazed, eyes brimming with tears, at the judge, 'It's all a dreadful, a terrible mistake. He,' she pointed a manicured paw at Fiston, 'is as innocent as any person in this room. You're making an appalling mistake!' Her voice faded as she focused on the judge, who now turned purple beneath his fur. He had risen to all four feet, eyes bulging.

'Silence!' screeched his Lordship, judicial tail erect. 'Who,' he spluttered, 'is that feline person? Who *is* she?' he demanded, looking around for the clerk of the court. 'I'll have her locked up for . . .' he groped for appropriate words, 'for . . . contempt,' he slavered. 'I will not tolerate such insolence in *my* court . . . such . . . disrespect. Bailiff, where are you? Arrest that . . . feline person!'

The object of his ire, the impulsive, aristocratic, white furred feline lost her commanding composure, cowered, and burst into tears.

'Sir, I didn't mean any disrespect . . . I know what you must

32

think. I come from a long line of er, semi-legal felines. My father was a policeman. But the truth is, sir . . . it's that Fiston is a *hero*, not a criminal. I can explain . . .'

'What,' spluttered the judge, 'are you babbling on about? You can't just interrupt the court! Who cares about your antecedents? A policeman! What . . . silence!'

'Sir, please let me explain. I loved that great tom hero before you on the stand,' the white apparition persisted while his lordship struggled for breath. 'I know him well. He must have been *out of his mind* to do anything wrong. That's,' she lowered her voice, 'if I may be allowed to tell the *whole* story.'

The judge glared, speechless. Somewhere in his ancient, foggy mind trembled a hoary twig of lechery. While struggling to regain his composure, he cast a salacious eye over her alluring figure. But before he could gather his judicial wits she went on.

'Our hearts should go out to him. All alone up there . . . my daddy would've said . . .'

'Your daddy! Harrrumph, SILENCE!' bellowed his Lordship, finally finding words. 'No more tomcat foolery. I don't care if your father made ice-cream or drove taxis! Sit down and be silent! This is not a skating rink!' Pleased with his display of knowledge of contemporaneous affairs, he caught the eye of the clerk of the court, a young tabby, and twitched his tail. The clerk smoothed her whiskers gracefully and dropped her eyes. Oh, that judge, she thought, he's a one, a lady's cat . . . at least when awake. Such charisma.

As he calmed down, the judge, overcome with drowsiness, yawned, stretched mightily, and composed his limbs. What *had* happened? He rubbed his nose absent-mindedly with a pudgy paw. He made a note in this book to remind himself to send the clerk a box of sardines.

'May it please your Lordship,' Felix the defending lawyer, exploiting the unexpected lull, stood, 'I request an adjournment.'

The gorgeous queen subsided into a round ball of smooth white fur. Felix signalled to her urgently to stay put. At last, a character witness!

'Yes, yes, I know what you want,' snapped his Lordship, his erotic reverie interrupted. 'We'll adjourn for twenty minutes. I want to see you two in my chambers.'

The lawyers, wigs wobbling on slippery, furry scalps, rose as one and bowed. The clerk of the court, taking her cue, called out, in a melodious meow, 'All rise for his Lordship.' The judge, gathering his robes around him, swept out, tail conspicuously erect. 'Now look here you two,' growled his Lordship to his legal colleagues sitting ill at ease on cushions in the judicial chambers. 'Was that . . . that planned? Are you . . . is she . . . going to be a witness? And how long do you two expect this case to run? I have an outing planned to hunt voles with an old friend and I promised my new missus I'd be away on circuit for no more than a week. Is this going on and on? What about it?'

'I can't be sure,' replied the prosecutor, gravely. 'This is a serious matter. We have to make an example. The accused's squandered eight lives! None of us, I trust, would dare to live so audaciously. No respect for tradition. He must pay or be punished severely. It may be that I'll demand that he relinquish his ultimate, his ninth life.'

'Oh, come now Boris,' protested Felix thinking fast, 'if I may be so bold, you're getting carried away again . . . come on! It so happens I have a surprise witness. But, I hasten to add, I did not arrange that scene in your lordship's court.'

'I should hope not. On the other hand, I believe we must be

fair and impartial,' interjected the judge, solemnly, suddenly overcome with ethos, not to mention the memory of the queen's white fur. 'After all that's what I, we, stand for . . . isn't it?'

Both lawyers stiffened. For an instant their eyes met. It was impossible not to conceal their astonishment. A fair, impartial . . . judge? Who did he think he was talking to?

Felix compressed his lips, hoping this thoughts weren't visible,

'Sir,' he purred, playing up to the bloated judge, 'we appreciate your great experience in these matters, but we would like to request an adjournment until tomorrow. I have to brief the new witness. And then see how it goes?'

'Oh, very well,' grumbled his lordship, 'have it your own way. But you don't have unlimited time! I get sort of . . . restless when I'm separated from my better half for too long.' He dismissed the lawyers with a curt nod and drifted off into another catnap.

The court had resumed the next day. The judge, for once, for a while, was awake.

'I would like to draw your attention to a certain matter that has arisen and may throw a new light on the proceedings . . . if my learned friend has no objection?' Felix nodded to Boris. 'I would like to call my next witness.'

'Objection!' responded Boris the prosecutor on principle,

'I thought we'd agreed to allow the witness's testimony?'

'Objection overruled,' the judge, eyeing the snow white witness, waved a legal paw.

'Boris and his knee jerk reactions . . .,' muttered the defence counsel in an aside to his junior. 'As for that judge, he's past it. He's about eighty cat years in the shade, playing the great jurist, and keeping up his act for show. New wife indeed . . . new bottle more likely. Anyway he's onto his eighth wife so that's nothing new. His rich family've bought him out of more than one scrape. Used to get blind drunk and fall over in court. Cut his head open once. No one did anything about it! "He's a great judge . . . when he's sober," the benchers claimed whenever he got himself in hot water. As a matter of fact he was known in his younger years as a wild cat. Used to pig out on scraps and caterwaul all night. Now, suddenly, he's the soul of rectitude. *It's all an act.* And we wonder why the public distrusts the legal profession?'

'Don't judges have mandatory retirement?'

'Hardly ever. The more senile the better. There's no profession so tolerant of, or overloaded with, demented dodderers. I'm sure their personal vets are brow beaten into keeping up pretences . . . certifying the old farts of sound mind. Should have a CAT scan, the lot. Anyway, to business. Get me that new cat. The one in court. She could be a crucial witness.'

'You're a touch cynical this morning,' smiled the junior, 'don't *you* want to be a judge?'

'Who wouldn't? All those perks . . . for life? Despite everything I've said, being a judge is an important milestone. A word of advice. In the beginning, if you want to get on, show willing. Be smart. Be visible. Get on TV shows. Write articles. Plagiarize precedents . . . you know . . . rewrite judgments and add a word or two. Talk about minority rights. But especially, write a book. Go over old cases, grey areas and precedents, and *voilà* . . . you'll be an acknowledged expert. In next to no time you'll get a judgeship. Writing a book, even a rehash, is a guarantee of success . . .'

'Especially if it's not read?'

'Especially if it's not read. And, if this were England, you'd be knighted, automatically.'

'*I* don't want to be a judge.'

'That's what you say now. What else is there? Haven't you noticed Boris' behaviour? He wears dark suits . . . for every case. Gravitas. That's it. Gravitas. He wants to win for the sake of his reputation.'

'Don't we all?'

'Winning's the game. Can't say I blame him. Four wives and twenty offspring to educate.'

At this point the judge intervened,

'How much longer do we have to wait, Felix? You've been consulting for long enough. We haven't all day!'

'Call the new witness.'

When all had seated, the beautiful white cat made her way to the witness stand. The judge lowered his judicial eyes and positively glowed at the cool kitty in the witness box.

'State your name and occupation,' commanded the clerk of the court.

'Carol,' she said quietly, 'no fixed address. I'm a designer, but out of work at present.'

'Let us return to the alleged incident,' Felix was standing casually, speaking without notes, paws dangling by his sides. 'What is you relationship to Fiston and what do you know about the alleged events?'

The atmosphere in the courtroom was by now heavy and stale. Oxygen was in short supply.

Fiston taking note of the sight of the learned judge, slumbering with eyes closed, found himself drifting off. In a few moments he was fast asleep. Soon he was dreaming. He was back at the beginning.

It was midsummer. The day was swelteringly hot. Nothing moved. A few squirrels flitted along the rails of the verandah at the rear of the house on Camel Street. Magpies had ceased their endless squawking and dozed in the branches of poplars at the rear of the house overlooking the ravine.

Fiston, a Russian Blue, sat, ears twitching silently, drowsing in the shade of the trees. His arch rival, Oscar, a canine of uncertain heritage, was fast asleep in his kennel. The grey cat surveyed his untrammelled domain. But his mind, even in his sleep, was not at rest. In fact it was seething with indignation as a vivid dream unfolded.

How could they? Years of obeisance and servility! All those generous offerings. What had he done to deserve such . . . abject humiliation? I'll get them, he thought in his dream and, for that matter, I'll fix it for Oscar at the same time. He awoke with a headache and glowered up at the sleeping magpies. Bloody birds. Nothing pleased him at that moment. He was in an extraordinarily foul mood. All the humans were out. He had no one to talk to. And he was famished. It was at least two hours since his last meal. He was a rapid metabolizer. For the twentieth time he wandered over to the French windows and gazed into the interior, where a dainty, blue grey kitten curled up under the table. He hissed with all his might. Bloody hell!

'Fiston, poor baby, you poor dear. Sitting all alone on the hot verandah.' Fiston gave a great start. It was one of the twins. Yegggh, thought Fiston, here we go. Trying to butter me up. Traitress! What about that Siamese?!'

'Oooh, how's baby? Hungry darling?'

'Piss off,' snarled Fiston, in his worst cat language.

'Did you hear that? He's answering. I wonder what he said?'

'Aw, God,' sighed Fiston, 'leave me in peace can't you?' He stalked off down the steps leading to the remnants of garden undamaged by Oscar's deposits. A confrontation with his arch enemy Oscar was preferable to gooey chatter. Fortunately Oscar was fast asleep and dreaming of chasing the neighbourhood cats en masse.

In a few moments silence descended. The human female disappeared. Fiston walked slowly around the house. For a while he sat, still in a reverie, grooming and basking in the sun. What to do? He looked up and noticed the window to the master bedroom was open. With an effortless bound he gained the sill. He paused to look around, then slithered stealthily through the invitingly open window. Without a moment's hesitation he dropped noiselessly onto the carpet in the bedroom then paused, frozen. Nothing happened. The room was spotless. Clarissa the cleaning lady had been busy. Fiston looked around for hidden danger. He sniffed the air for trouble. Not a hint of human scent. He stalked over to the bed and with a smooth bound landed on the duvet. Forbidden territory! He sat there quietly for a few seconds savouring his adventure. This was no cat's land for certain. A delicious thrill of excitement coursed through his body. No cat's land! A surge of reckless courage consumed him, displacing all common sense. His previous disaffected humour evaporated. What could be the *very worst* thing he could do . . . and get even with that stupid, silly, miserable Siamese? And perhaps, for that matter, bloody Oscar?

He paced up and down the duvet. Then, his mind made up, he rose high on all fours, arched his spine, and let his tail face the pillows. At that moment he caught sight of himself in a floor-to-ceiling mirror. He turned slowly to admire his profile. Not bad, he thought. Then, with infinite precision, he backed his derriere closer to the pillows. He was now poised over the very centre of the pillow. Fiston began to strain and grunt. He wiggled his hips and in a second it was all over. Without a backward glance he leaped onto the window sill and made a lightning exit, leaving behind on the bed a steaming, semi-liquid gift.

Oscar stirred in his sleep and woke irritably. A cheeky magpie perched on his kennel was busily pecking at a large morsel of Oscar's breakfast.

'Get away you . . . bird,' he barked, and dashed, ineffectually, after his black and white avian tormentor. He'd never make it, but had to try. Just at that moment he heard, in the distance, the sound of the family four wheel drive vehicle returning.

Must greet them outside, he thought. Oscar galloped off to the foot of the steps leading onto the verandah. In a scrambling rush he rounded the corner only to come face to face with Fiston. For a second the two stood inert, face to face. This was Oscar's territory. Fiston, desperate to get away from the scene of his misdemeanour, refused to give ground. Taken aback by the cat's unexpected boldness, Oscar hesitated, looked sideways, affected to ignore Fiston, and circled past. The front door banged shut. He was too late. Bloody cat.

'Edward! *Come here!*'

'What is it?'

'Come here!'

The middle-aged man dropped the two large suitcases in the front hall and walked slowly upstairs. He was exhausted and irritable. They had been driving for eight hours, non-stop.

'What's the fuss? We've only just . . .' The rest of his sentence was lost as he opened the door to the bedroom. The little Siamese scurried past and shot down the stairs.

'What is it?'

At first he did not recognize the substance on the bed his gibbering wife was pointing at. On closer inspection he identified what was a foul smelling lump of faeces.

'Revolting! Who did it? One of the children?'

'Don't be so stupid, Edward. It must have been the cat.'

'Which one?' A thought struck him, 'It couldn't have been Oscar, could it?'

'Who do you think just ran out of the room?'

'That bloody Siamese. I'll do her in.'

'No you won't. You always over-react. It's not her fault. She's not trained. And you didn't actually see her do it. Could've been Fiston.'

'Over-react? Not trained?' words failed him as he spluttered, 'we, we . . . drive all that way . . . we arrive worn out, ready to drop into bed . . . and then that! Not her fault? You've gone dotty, woman.'

'Edward . . .,' a warning tone crept into her voice, 'you're being unreasonable.'

'Unreasonable! *This is too much.* A cat craps on the bed and I . . . I am unreasonable? What is this . . . a house, or a litter box?'

'Don't make such a fuss, Edward.'

'Who's making the fuss?' he asked, reasonably.

'It'll be washed and be as good as new.'

The male human stalked off, scowling as he searched around for wayward felines. He descended the stairs with a face of thunder. In the front hall by the suitcases he came upon Fiston, lying playfully on his back, purring, and wagging his paws in the air. An entrancing display of cat good humour. A clear

41

invitation to play.

'Bugger off,' said the man and, to emphasize his suggestion, helped Fiston on his way with the toe of a shoe. At that moment the twins entered the front door. Fiston, seizing his opportunity, let out an indignant 'Meeeooow!'

'Dad! What are you doing? We *saw* you. Poor darling Fiston. How could you? You hate him, don't you?'

'Why do you two creep around . . . everywhere? Do you know what he did?' spluttered their father. 'He . . . he . . . crapped on the bed!'

'On the bed! It couldn't have been Fiston. How do you know it wasn't the Siamese, or Oscar? He's always hanging around outside the bedroom.'

Their mother's voice floated down from the upper landing. 'Your father's just being his usual grouchy self. If animals don't know any better, he should.'

'What exactly do you mean by that?'

His wife didn't reply. Around the corner, Fiston, grinning cat-like to himself, paused in his pseudo-flight to overhear. But what he heard was not exactly what he had expected, or hoped for! An unexpected twist had developed. The idiot female humans were *condoning* his crime. That bloody, lucky brat, the Siamese had been exonerated! All his brilliant plotting . . . wasted. Somehow they knew it was him, Fiston. All to no avail! Fiston began to simmer and grind his teeth with impotent rage.

'Oh, hell,' he growled, aloud, 'there's no justice in this world . . . no justice at all, for me.'

And, adding insult to injury, the male human thing spotted him. Under the correct assumption that it had been Fiston who'd committed the dastardly deed, he started chasing him, ignominiously off the porch, with a broom! Fiston was forced to retreat, hastily, into awful Oscar's precinct. Luckily Oscar was out of sight. Everything was going wrong in his nightmarish dream.

Chapter 4

Fiston Reminisces

Fiston woke with a start to hear his name being called. He shook his head, cleared his mind, and gazed around. Where *was* he? How long had he been dreaming? He looked up to find all eyes in the court were on him.

'Fiston,' Boris the prosecutor, his brow furrowed in pseudo-bewilderment, was speaking, '. . . may I have your attention? Would you explain to us exactly what you had in mind? I have great difficulty following your explanations.'

'I'm sorry, I'm not making myself clear again,' replied Fiston with a straight face, 'it's quite difficult to recall a dream-state,' and added, with solemn emphasis, 'it's *very* hard indeed. Have you ever tried to recall a dream . . . in detail?'

The prosecutor stared but made no reply.

Fiston, playing for time, was doing his best to construct a plausible framework for his explanation. He'd always been good at thinking on his feet.

'Ey, wazzat? *What* did you say?' interrupted the judge, as he emerged briefly from his torpor. It occurred to him that Fiston had been poking fun at his Holy Cow, the law. *Anything* that might be construed as the least disrespectful of legal niceties, especially under *his* nostrils, was the equivalent of waving a red rag to an enraged bull. Activity in the court paused while his lordship adjusted his judicial wig. It was of no concern that he'd been asleep for a while. It had been his immutable conviction that veneration of judges was directly proportional to the amount of umbrage taken and displayed in court, whatever the circumstances.

Felix, the defending lawyer, groaned softly. God knows, he thought, what was passing through that atrophied cerebrum. Unfortunately his client, bent on developing a theme of diminished responsibility, was becoming over-confident. There was nothing to be done. He hoped for the best.

'I apologize. I should answer questions,' said Fiston contritely, swivelling to face the scowling judge, 'it's not my place to ask. Is it?'

'Harmmmph,' muttered the judge.

'I was, in my ignorant way, attempting to illustrate trouble with my memory of dreams. Occasionally I cannot make myself understood,' and added, under his breath, 'to old farts like you, sir.'

'Well, speak up,' groused the judge, suspiciously, and lapsed into a semi-stupor, his displeasure subsiding. A gentle snore broke the stillness in the room.

The prosecutor, head bent over his files, however, had heard Fiston's sotto voce remark and straightened his back to face the cheeky witness. His expression, like any good lawyer's, was inscrutable. That cat'll pay dearly for his cheek, he vowed,

'For the second time sir . . . answer my question.'

'Would you mind repeating it?'

'What . . . on the night of the er, event, were your intentions . . . motives? You admitted you knew you were off limits. What were you planning to do there?'

'Was I? Was it real?'

'Oh, don't let's play games,' snapped the prosecutor wearily, turning to the snoring judge. 'His memory fails at convenient moments.' He looked enquiringly at his lordship, but the latter was in dreamland, breathing stertorously, eyes shut.

Fiston persisted, 'I wouldn't dream of playing games, not here! I believe I told you that at *that* time my mind was . . . not working. I wasn't in control of my actions. I have islands of memory of what *might* have occurred. I don't know if it's true at all. There were, I understand, no witnesses.'

The prosecutor, paused for what seemed like hours, scanning piles of notes,

'On the night of the 30th, er, evidence of a faecal nature was discovered in, shall we say, unusual, incriminating circumstances and places. We are led to conclude that, if it was *not* the Siamese . . . your own words . . . then it follows you were responsible. It did happen. Who else could have done it?'

Fiston sighed, 'I've already told you. I *think* I did it. But, equally, I now realize I was *out of my mind* . . . at that moment. I was in an automatic, uncomprehending state. I had no control over my instincts. In my dream I was protesting. If I had been sane, or awake, I wouldn't have done it. I must've been dreaming. Or was I in a dream state?'

Boris let out an exasperated, legal groan, nothing was clear.

'So you would have us believe . . .,'

Felix, the defence attorney, rose with studied smoothness, outacting for the moment, his learned colleague.

'M'lord,' he turned to the judge whose heavy lidded eyes were flicking open and shut, 'I can't see where this is leading. We have already established, with Doctor von Straws' evidence . . .'

'Quite so,' said the judge. 'Boris, I think you've belaboured the point. Let's move on. Have you any other questions for this witness?'

The prosecutor, taken out of his stride, spluttered, 'Very well, as your lordship pleases, I will move on.' He turned to Fiston, 'One question. Do you admit you defecated on the duvet?'

'I don't remember,' answered Fiston, the grey eminence, dreamily, 'it's possible. If I *thought* I did it . . . a symbolic act . . . was I there? Or in a dream? I'm confused . . .'

'So it seems.'

'Can't you see my difficulty?'

'No, I'm afraid not.'

'Whoever did it, it was an uncivilized gesture.'

'We agree on that.'

'But in dreams don't we . . . try to act out secret desires?'

'You're the expert, it seems.'

'I think that *the balance of my mind was disturbed*. I simply don't know . . . I'm lost.'

'Aren't we all,' sneered the prosecutor. 'How convenient it is to have developed this amnesia. Would you call it hysterical amnesia or malingering amnesia?'

The judge hearing the interchange, pricked up his ears, 'Amnesia? How d'you spell that?'

'A.M.N.E.S.I.A.,' enunciated Boris helpfully, 'H.Y.S.T.E.R.I.C.A.L. That's what Doctor von Straws diagnosed. Fiston was suffering from . . . *hysterical amnesia*. Or in other words, a fugue state.'

The judge wrote down 'hysterical amnesia', and sat back, satisfied at last.

The grey cat smiled inwardly. Thank you for that help, m'lord. The jury noticed the judge's questions, exchanged looks and all wrote down 'Hysterical Amnesia'.

'No more questions, m'lord.' Boris resumed his seat, irritated. One remark too many . . . and from his bloody lordship.

'Counsel for the defence?' The judge, remembering protocol, looked enquiringly at Felix the defence counsel for a response.

The latter rose and bent over his notes.

'M'lord,' he began, gravely, 'it's clear that my client is, was, ill. *Temporary insanity*. His medical condition has been explained by Doctor von Straws, a leading forensic psychiatrist. His actions must be viewed in the light of Hysterical Amnesia. That is his defence.'

'It may be that this trial will have far reaching medico-legal er' overtones? Set a precedent?' The judge preened and looked toward the ceiling. Headlines appeared in his head,

'Judge Tobias Catz defines new precedent.'

Fiston's mind began to wander . . .

Fiston sat stoic and alone on his favourite perch, the flower pot by the front door. The weather had changed. The sky was heavy, grey and drizzling; Oscar, as usual, was barking his head off. From within the house he could hear the mewing of the garrulous Siamese displaced person.

What a life, he thought mournfully, I'm sick of everything. I can't see a light at the end of the tunnel. He stared into the gloom with unseeing eyes. It's obvious, he thought bitterly, I'm no longer wanted. Ah well, he sighed heavily, rose, arched his back and strolled to the house next door where he sat on the front porch. But the place was deserted. With increasing gloom he rose once more and began to walk down the street. He had no direction in mind. The innermost depths of his feline soul were churning with melancholic pain. He wished only to lose himself in some distant, silent void. Suicide by walking. Before long he was many blocks away. He kept going on and on into the looming dusk. Soon street lights came on. Doggedly Fiston plodded on. The neighbourhood was now unfamiliar. Something . . . some mechanism . . . in his brain was guiding him. He walked on, an automaton, a feline robot immersed in self pity.

'Hullo handsome,' a seductive, melodious voice, from somewhere under a hedge filled his ears. Fiston paused. Who was it?

'I say, gorgeous, who are you? How come I've not seen you before?' A snow white queen stepped daintily from behind the hedge. Fiston sniffed the air. Her perfume was heavy . . . inviting, intoxicating. The remains of his shattered hormonal system stirred. His mind became suffused and confused with vague memories.

'Hullo,' he answered, nonchalantly, trying to activate atavistic instincts, 'I don't usually come this way. Anyway, how come you . . . how come you're allowed out so late?' Fiston looked suspiciously around for other cat bodies. It seemed probable that there might be a strange thug tom lurking about with such a delectable prize in view. Was she a trap?

'I got out through the basement window . . . and escaped,' she answered. 'It was stifling inside the house. Bloody kids, pestering me. Dressing me in ridiculous human clothing. Me, a mature queen. I want something better out of life. I want to live!' She looked coyly at him. 'Time I started living. How about it, handsome? Would you like to examine my back?'

Fiston was taken aback by her directness. Despite his recent attack of the glums he felt his pulse rising. A strange, pleasant sensation began to swirl in his mind and through his body. He turned and casually approached the snow white feline.

'What's your name kid?' he asked, huskily.

'Carol,' repeated the queen, and proceeded to rub her face and sides against his cheek. Fiston's response was instantaneous. He leaped around and embraced her, while gently nipping the back of her neck. He'd forgotten his history. Primeval instinct had taken over. With a soft sigh the queen sank to her haunches and moaned. Fiston let a short, weird, almost human cry of triumph. A cry that, through the centuries, had issued from his antecedents. But an instant of passion transfigured into a mournful lament. Monstrously mortified, he realized his body had failed him. Carol waited patiently. After a while she curled onto her back and gazed into Fiston's yellow orbits.

'What's wrong honey?' she meowed. Then sensing something unusual said, softly, 'Don't worry . . . darling it's all right.'

'I'm sorry,' muttered Fiston, 'I can't help it. You're so beautiful. I forgot what those bloody humans had done to me. My spirit's willing . . . you're madly attractive . . . but there's nothing there. Can we be friends . . . could we?' He looked in forlorn appeal at her.

'Oh sure,' she replied, her heart melting, 'not to worry. I was too fresh anyway. Do I intimidate you?'

Fiston looked away. He felt himself warming beneath his coat of grey fur, 'No you don't . . . it's not you. It's not *that.* You see, when I was a helpless kitten . . .'

'Oh, dear, *I do understand*,' said Carol, softly. 'You poor dear! Don't fret, of course we can be friends. I'll prove it. I'll show you. Forever.'

'How?'

'I'll go off anywhere . . . with you. We can live together. I won't miss what I don't know. It's not everything.'

Fiston, tears welling in his eyes, walked over to Carol, gave her a long, loving lick and stood aside as she went ahead, tail erect. Together they walked down the street.

Fitfully flickering street lights were coming on. The memory of his recent débâcle faded. Fiston's step lightened. Before him stretched a new vista. A new life! Freedom! No painful memories!

Chapter 5

A New Life

'Fiston, now's the time to tell me about yourself,' purred Carol, the voluptuous queen. They were languishing under a ramshackle porch at the front of an ancient, deserted building where the two strays had settled for the night. 'I have to know more about you.'

'Well, okay. But I don't want to sound too . . . discontented. I don't like to whinge,' said Fiston bravely, 'but . . . since you ask, I'll let you have a glimmer of my past.' He reclined, splendidly relaxed, full length, head resting on a front paw. Ah, he thought, this is great. For once to have *someone's* undivided attention. No intrusive, babbling girls to push me aside. Drawing a deep breath he launched into his, by now, oft rehearsed narrative, punctuated at strategic intervals with appropriate sighs and pauses.

Despite Fiston's eloquence, Carol's eyelids began to droop. Fiston stared at her with a mixture of fond affection and consternation. Was it possible that he could be so tedious? There was a message for him in this. Cry and you cry alone, laugh and the world laughs with you! Where'd he heard that? Well, he thought, I enjoy a challenge. My main asset's my flexibility. Tomorrow . . . tomorrow will be time enough to assume a new, better, stronger personality. Enough of hissing, spitting, and impotent grumbling. From this day forward, he resolved, my character'll be laconic, aloof, and mixed with a strong, mysterious reticence. I know exactly what's needed . . . a Clint Eastwood charisma perhaps? For a while he pondered the implications of a character transformation. Who else might be a suitable role model? A feline Tarzan? Felix the Cat? Robin Fiston-Hood? Tommy Lee Fiston-Jones? Carol's drowsiness was infectious and he began to yawn mightily. He'd think of something in the morning. Flexing his claws he stretched his aching muscles and was soon fast asleep. In a few minutes he was dreaming of heroic events in which, among others, the wretched Siamese and that cad, Oscar, played degrading roles. Little did Fiston dream of the curious twists of fate that lay in store.

Dawn was breaking when Fiston stirred. The sky in the east was covered with pale, orange streaked, giant bubbles of grey clouds. Hypersensitive hearing detected the faintest of squeaks emanating from somewhere below the rotting floor boards. He rose without a sound, and slithered sinuously to the edge of the ancient verandah. With practised ease he inched his lithe, elegant shape under decomposing floor joists. The sounds ceased abruptly, but he sensed he was near his breakfast. He waited in breathless silence until he detected a soft rustle. Gathering his muscles into a coiled spring, Fiston locked his toenails onto the boards. With a tremendous, encircling rush he scooped up a petrified field mouse. The mouse let out a forlorn, squeak as its soul sped to rodent heaven. Mouth full, Fiston walked coolly back to Carol still blissfully asleep, and dropped the morsel beneath her gently undulating nostrils. The scent of the meal woke her instantly.

'Oooh, how lovely, breakfast in bed. Oh, you are good to me Fiston,' she smiled and forthwith set to. Fiston sat back, glowing with gratification, and groomed his tail region. He paused to study his companion. Carol, eating with unlady-like voracity, consumed the mouse in two minutes flat. She spared the entrails, leaving them, a neat bundle, on the breakfast floor.

'Have a bite, dear Fiston.'

'No thanks,' replied Fiston, suppressing a shudder. He was ravenous but detested tripe. Besides, he was in the process of developing a new, independent, image. 'I'll have something later,' he added, loftily.

Carol stared at him for several seconds, huge, green eyes wide.

'Where's my baby?' whined the older of the twins – by fifteen minutes. She clumped crossly through the open front door. 'What's he *doing*? It's been two whole days. He's nowhere to be seen. He must be *totally* lonely and massively *starving*, poor baby. It's all your fault,' she added, addressing her parents. Ingrained in her mind was the notion that food was love, ever since her obese, slow witted grandmother had pronounced that 'food was everything. Food was love.'

'Everyone,' announced her Scottish grandmother for the umpteenth time, 'needs reserves. The best sort's fat, plenty of it,' emphasizing her statement by running her plump dimpled hands over her ample form. 'Fat's good for you . . . just in case you fall sick. We, in the old country, ate properly, porridge, fried bread, bacon . . . we *never* worried about green veggies or fruit. Look at us . . . aren't we healthy?'

The male looked up from his newspaper with ill concealed distaste, 'No doubt that explains why so many of your

54

countrymen die young. It's a fact that the Scots' diet's about the worst in the world. Personally I wouldn't feed it even to Fiston, or a snake.' The twins' father's delight was to contradict the old nag's primitive theories. But she was not to be defeated.

'Rubbish!' she invariably responded, with finality.

At the mention of Fiston's name the twins renewed their whining.

'Where is baby?'

'You can stick to porridge and fried bread, Grandma, but not for us. This isn't Scotland.'

'My generation knew what was good for them. Don't you contradict me.'

'Maybe if they bathed occasionally that would have helped,' muttered the beleaguered male.

'What?'

'Nothing.'

The thought of Fiston *sans* grub was almost too much for omnivorous teenage minds to bear. 'What's he going to do?'

'Good riddance, if you ask me,' grinned Edward the embattled male, burying his head in his newspaper. 'One cat in the house's more than enough. I have no space anywhere. Cats, girls, and nothing but blather. You never fed the wretched animal. The irony is that it's been my unenviable job to see he doesn't starve. Just like I end up doing our washing up. You're always out gallivanting about and using this place like a boarding house. And who, may I point out, pays his vet's bills?'

'Edward,' snapped his wife, the alpha female, 'stop whinging. Who cooks the meals, who makes your sandwiches, who . . . perhaps you should learn to cook?'

'Okay. Okay. It's all my fault. You're always right.'

The Siamese leaped onto the breakfast table and began to

nibble leftover bacon scraps.

'Get *off!* . . . Wretched cat!' snapped the man, wielding the newspaper, whereupon the Siamese playfully charged the newspaper and began to paw, kittenishly, his fingers wrapped around the editorial page, 'I don't have any space!'

'Dad! You're awful. You hate cats, don't you! You hate us. It's no use pretending.' It was partly true.

'I hate you? What nonsense. You can be a pain, but,' he added hastily, 'no one's perfect. I'm not. As for cats . . . just some cats. I don't really mind this one. If it comes to that Fiston's just about bearable . . . sometimes. Anyway, if he comes back, *you* feed him, *you* pay his bills.'

'You hate cats.'

The Siamese, bored, wandered over to the bay window in the sitting room. I wonder if Fiston left because of me? she thought, What did I do? she pondered, experiencing a twinge of guilt. What can I do to bring him back? If only I could *prove* to him I was nice. Not just a pretty face. The Siamese curled into a ball and continued to stare through a window with bright blue eyes. She was actually beginning to miss grouchy old Fiston. Far better than that grouchy old human.

Fiston and Carol – her freshly caught, delectable breakfast finished – completed their respective ablutions, and for good measure licked each other all over. The morning was chilly and damp. A floating mist distorted the outlines of the dilapidated buildings. Sunbeams silhouetted once proud, now ghostly structures. Flickering motes of light floated in beams that bathed their bodies, casting curious, misshapen shadows on the ground.

'I'll be glad to get out of here,' Carol gave an involuntary shudder.

'You'd better get used to this, dearie. It's safe, really,' said Fiston, scanning around. 'We're equipped for survival. We're superior beings, aren't we? I mean, consider our senses; eyes, noses, and ears, all superb. No one, nothing, can take us by surprise. We live by our special senses.'

No sooner had he said this than, rounding a corner, they came face to face with a large, unfriendly, Rottweiler.

'So much for our superior senses,' shouted Carol, breathlessly, as they scampered hastily away and leaped headlong through an empty apartment block window.

'He took me by surprise. I wasn't concentrating,' muttered Fiston, glaring out the window, fur erect. 'Rotten Rottweiler. Bully. Got nothing better to do. Hey you,' he hissed, 'get off. Frighten someone your own size. Stupid dog!'

The dog leaped, barked and slavered furiously, its teeth snapping with alarmingly powerful clashes below the open window. Carol sank to the floor and retreated to a far wall. Eventually the dog, spent by his continuous, aggressive posturing, trotted off, not before marking the territory with lifted leg.

As soon as the coast was clear, more or less convinced he was invulnerable in his acquired, heroic personality, Fiston ventured out to sniff the air cautiously. Satisfied he turned and beckoned to his companion. Carol followed, a wave of warm affection, which she recognized as partly erotic, passed through and rippled her snow white fur.

'So, mon brave, Fiston . . .'

'It's nothing.'

'I feel safe with you.'

57

Chapter 6

Oscar's Lament

The day dawned muggy and oppressively overcast. Humid air, almost tangible with moisture, floating in low clouds, seemed poised to coalesce into rain drops. A group of squirrels, safe in Fiston's absence, gathered food at great speed while sprinting with miraculous agility along a highway of wires that conveyed electricity, television signals, and unending telephone conversations, into the house on the ravine.

Oscar, ears drooping, rambled along the perimeter of the back yard searching for something, he knew not what. For once his tormentors, the wretched magpies, were silent. It had been many, many days since he'd last come across Fiston. Weird, he thought, I ought to hate him, and here I am wondering what's up with him? Is that dumb cat alive?

In the distance he imagined he heard a lone coyote howling defiance. Automatically he responded with a staccato burst of barks that reached, at least, an ear shattering 120 decibels. The din rattled the walls of the house for minutes on end without a break, until the dominant member of Oscar's pack, the formidable alpha female, emerged to put a stop to the racket.

She walked to the edge of the balcony, arms held stiffly by her sides, took a deep breath and, shouting, at full pitch, tried to make herself heard over Oscar's racket,

'Oscar! . . . Oscar! Shut up!' she bellowed, shaking with effort. The message got through. Oscar slunk sheepishly towards his kennel wagging his tail in a gesture of subjugation. For a while he lay there curled up and gazing glumly out of the narrow passage to his bedroom. But not for long. Soon, hot and restless, he resumed his patrol of the boundary of a territory that reached into a wooded ravine at the back of the house. A sturdy metal chain link fence marked the limits of his undisputed realm.

Just then a pale, languid youth with two pony sized St Bernards in tow appeared ambling at a leisurely pace along a path below the link fence. In an instant all Hell broke loose as Oscar hurled himself onto the unyielding steel barrier in a remarkable and admirable imitation of ungovernable rage and menace. The enormous, passing canines, each of whom was several times his size and weight, stopped in their tracks. A delirious mock battle ensued as all the dogs hurled canine insults while simultaneously displaying frightful rows of colossal fangs. Oscar knew his business. The fence was slim but unyielding. The transparent barrier was strong enough to contain a herd of maddened buffalo. The renewed cacophony brought forth the female leader of Oscar's pack for the second time that afternoon. Her brows were knitted and her lips pursed.

'Oscar, you . . . ridiculous animal . . . shut up! Oscar! OSCAR!' she roared hoarsely, at the top of her considerable voice. But Oscar had gone deaf and continued the frenzied pseudo-battle with the St Bernards. Eventually the pale youth managed to drag his enormous pets away and set off down the path to find someone else to aggravate. As they disappeared into the ravine Oscar, puffed up by his latest triumph, kicked up a fine cloud of dust with his hind legs while holding his brakes with front feet firmly planted in the soil. Tossing a final, deafening chorus of barks into the air, he walked briskly back to the house to mount the flight of stairs that led to the balcony. There he sat scowling, his blood up, for several minutes until, slowly, he calmed down. After a while he turned his gaze inward to the living room and searched in vain for his arch enemy, Fiston. But there was no Fiston. No one else to intimidate.

The next day Oscar rose early and made a half hearted pretence of chasing off the thieving magpies that monotonously surrounded his breakfast dish. Once more he mounted the stairs to search the interior of the human dwelling. What he saw was a dejected family listlessly feeding their faces. Fiston was not to be seen. Oscar raised a tentative paw and scraped the glass of the French windows. One of the surly twins looked up.

'Oh! It's only Oscar,' her petulant voice broke with disappointment, 'I suppose I'd better feed him.' A thought struck her. She turned to her twin busy eating with elbows spread-eagled, nudging her father's newspaper. 'D'you think that slime Oscar might've frightened poor baby away? Sent him off . . . for ever? Fiston's hiding somewhere, afraid to come back!'

The irritable second-in-command of the pack, nudged his surly offspring's elbow out of the way, emerged from the newspaper, and let out a sardonic laugh,

'*Oscar . . . scare Fiston?* Not bloody likely. That cat'd frighten the back feet off the poor old boy. Oscar's all bark and no bite.'

'Piffle. Dog owners always say that. I know better. Every dog's a danger. All those fangs,' remarked the commander-in-chief, the alpha female. 'I have been, more than once, chased and bitten by a neighbour's pet, your friend, a dog. I've been terrified of dogs ever since.'

'Man's best friend? Come on. Not all dogs are the same. Not

all humans are.'

'I simply refuse to like dogs. They are weapons. Potentially lethal. So aggressive!'

'I said, not all dogs. You're a specieist. You could be right about some dogs. Little dogs or oversized ones. *I*, for one, wouldn't tussle with a St Bernard. You know Oscar's different. He's a lovely dog. He's never bitten anything. He's never been in a real fight, unless it's his act with another dog safely on the other side of the fence. Like those St Bernards. He's much too smart to get into a fight. Anyway, we've all seen that king of the castle cat Fiston beat up on Oscar.'

'Fiston's gone for ever,' sobbed a twin, her voice shaking, 'my baby'll never come back.'

'Your baby? He's not your baby. Anyway, mark my words, he'll be back. I remember when he followed us for miles across town. When we moved house. Just wait. When he's hungry enough he'll be back. Cupboard love. No loyalty in cats. And in any case, we've got a cat. You've been neglecting that . . . that . . . Siamese thing.'

'You hate Fiston don't you?' It was really a statement.

'Enough,' groaned the under leader from under his newspaper. 'Don't let's play that old record again. For your information I think Fiston, as cats go, is not all bad. Spoilt, lazy, manipulative maybe. A bit like you lot. I haven't forgotten his crapping habits. I think I'll go to my study. Can't have breakfast in peace.'

'How do you know it was him?'

'Deduction, my dear Watson. It was revenge. Cats're like that. Fiston was just bloody jealous. He thinks he's the leader of this pack, whereas Oscar has enough intelligence to see I am.'

'Is that so?' responded the alpha female, mockingly, 'In that case you may make your own supper, do your own laundry, and take the dog for a walk while you're at it. The exercise will do you both good. Don't forget the washing up.'

'I never do!'

A morose twin rose from the table, leaving her dishes, magazines, and paper napkin to fend for themselves, and left the room to feed Oscar.

Oscar, seeing her head for the stairs, sensing food and a tidbit of attention, thundered down the outside stairs to the garden where he sat waiting patiently by the ground level back door. The door opened and the glum faced twin, her mouth slack and open, emerged bearing his rations. Almost before she'd locked the door behind her Oscar had finished the meal. Age old instincts, derived from wolf ancestors, buried in his genes gloried in Oscar's habit of gulping food as fast as possible. I wonder, he thought, lapping his water, what's happened to that bloody cat? He was beginning to feel more than a trifle lost without someone to focus on or to hate. He was blown about by a combination of emotions he found somewhat novel and unnerving. He wondered if he might be going daft and trotted down to the fence to bark deafeningly into the space over the ravine. Cheered slightly by this activity he strolled back to his kennel for a morning nap. Time enough to look out for Fiston.

As the days slipped by a deepening gloom settled over the house on the ravine. Once or twice the miserable twins forgot to feed Oscar. Something's got to be done about this, thought Oscar, his stomach rumbling, if only for the sake of regular meals. He resisted the idea that he might actually miss that impossible cat. At that moment the new arrival, the Siamese, entered his territory from the far side. Oscar, brows knitted, stared in disbelief. Fiston would not've dared to invade *his* territory so blatantly!

The Siamese, unfazed, arched her back and approached Oscar in a series of stiff legged, lateral leaps, like a prancing springbok. Oscar, baffled, stood his ground, a menacing growl emanated from deep inside his throat. A ridge of fur rose along his spine. To his amazement the Siamese paused and, instead of backtracking, began to hiss. For moments the two stood facing each other frozen in time. Then Oscar pulled out all stops and barked as he'd never barked before. The Siamese flattened her ears. The noise rattled and hurt her eardrums. She began to retreat. This was a serious mistake. No one backs off when faced by an angry dog. Oscar, sensing victory, lurched forward, teeth bared, ready to engulf the cat whole. A twin emerged from the house in the nick of time.

'OSCAR!' she shrieked. 'You scoundrel! I saw that! Oscar . . . stop it!'

Whatever Oscar had had in mind vanished in a flash. His head sagged. He shut his jaws, lowered his retracted lips to hide his canines, and began to wuffle, simultaneously wagging an hypocritical tail. This usually worked with the deputy leader of the pack. But the twin was, not unusually for her, hard, cross, and immune to reason. To Oscar she was another opinionated cat person. She was one of that special, illogical breed, a female teenager with an unjustified, high regard for herself and her views. Nothing could touch her mind.

'Back to your kennel . . . you rotten hound! and stay there! Leave the kitty alone! You awful . . . dog! It's all your fault Fiston's gone. I hate you!' It was her tone more than anything else which registered in Oscar's mind. No use, he thought, I can't win. The fact that he'd probably frightened off countless burglars seemed to count for naught. An invading parasite in the shape of a blue-grey furry thing with a long tail carried more weight. It was all too unfair. He couldn't begin to protest. How or where to start? Perhaps . . . perhaps, one day when *he* was gone he'd be appreciated? I doubt it, he thought, disconsolately and retreated into his kennel. This was not a world for the likes of dogs. Little did Oscar suspect that soon startling events would overshadow his present difficulties.

Chapter 7

The Taxidermist Strikes

It was summer. Carol and Fiston dozed fitfully in the warmth of a seaside sun. They had dined superbly off a meal of scraps scrounged from dustbins at the rear of a rundown sea front hotel grandly entitled *Alphen House*.

Fate, in the shape of an elderly, arthritic, taxidermist was about to invade their existence. That morning the lugubrious animal stuffer had managed to wreck an extremely lucrative, special project. Madame Zoë Beck, a wealthy widow with more wealth than taste, had entrusted him with the task of embalming her favourite toy, a Russian Blue of similar senescence.

As the result of faulty technique the Russian Blue emerged an unlikely orange-pink colour. To make matters worse the cat configuration had disappeared, leaving behind a caricature of a feline outline. Not for the first time had the taxidermist's skill in maintaining a likeness of the defunct animal failed. An all-night poker game with equally decrepit cronies – a trio that consisted of a butcher, a baker, and a disbarred lawyer – had done such artistic attributes as he possessed no good at all. Things looked bad that morning when he viewed the entity that seemed to have materialized overnight on the slab in his workshop. To make matters worse a particularly foul stench rose almost palpably from the stuffed carcass. It was not a success.

For a long time he sat in heavy silence viewing the latest disaster. The vivid image of five hundred large bank notes passing before his eyes produced a sudden inspiration. Why not? Another cat! he thought. Fatso Beck would never know. She wouldn't be able to tell the difference, in her perpetual alcoholic haze, between her cat and any other Blue Russian.

The taxidermist went by the name of Willy Wilson – which was most peculiar because he pronounced the 'W' as 'V' in a guttural German accent. After he'd left his native Germany Wilhelm Wilhemstein had had the foresight to switch his name to Willi Holdstone and, when that proved difficult to pronounce, a year later to Willy Wilson. When sceptical acquaintances quizzed him about his antecedents and his original name, he was able to answer, deadpan and truthfully, 'Willi Holdstone'.

In any event Willy shut up his shop and made for the rear where he kept an ancient Austin van painted with faded gold lettering on the sides,

'Keep-Your-Pet-Forever Services, Ltd. Prop: W. Wilson, F.T.S., Esq.'

Wilson, as was appropriate for his profession, was permanently outfitted in a black raincoat over a crumpled blue serge suit, a black Stetson-type hat, and battered brown boots. Beneath his bald pate his face sported a bushy Kaiser Wilhelm moustache and steel rimmed, heavily tinted, trifocal glasses. Permanently compressed, thin lips concealed an array of decaying teeth, mostly incisors. Despite his general air of physical decrepitude he possessed keen senses. His eyesight was magnificent.

Willy Wilson drove slowly down the main road and headed for the sea front. He was familiar with the rows of seedy boarding houses that alternated with broken-down 'residential hotels'. One of these, *Alphen House*, was the setting for poker games held on weekends. Each building was more shabby than the next. He drove the length of the sea-front boulevard, made an acute U turn and backtracked slowly along the back alley of the buildings. There were no cats to be seen, let alone anything resembling a Russian Blue. His spirits began to sink. The brain wave had been a good one but it had been wishful thinking. That is, until he again drove, more slowly, for a final survey, along the cluttered alley at the rear of the buildings. There were cats. But not of the right sort! The rattling approach scattered scores of moth-eaten, feral cats. An occasional mangy canine hissed and slunk off at his approach.

Finally, two houses from *Alphen House*, Willy Wilson parked his car, reached into a pocket and brought out his lunch of yesterday, a stale sardine sandwich. He pondered the situation. The strong fishy smell gave him the second brain wave of the day.

He left the car parked by a '**Strictly No Parking**' sign and began to retrace his passage on foot. His route brought him to the kitchens at the rear of *Alphen House*. And there, *mirabile dictu*, he saw, basking in the sun, of all things, a sleek Russian Blue side by side with a snow white, long haired companion. He couldn't believe his luck. Approaching on tip toe, brown boots squeaking eerily, he paused by a garden shed overlooking his prey. The Russian Blue flicked an ear in his direction. It was clear to Willy Wilson that he'd been spotted. But that was part of his design. Squatting on his haunches in the shade of the shed he dropped the sardine sandwich a few feet ahead, in line with the dozing cats. In a few seconds the white cat's nostrils began to twitch and she raised her head to gaze with greeny-grey eyes in the direction of the aroma. Her movements disturbed the Russian Blue.

'What is it?' asked Fiston.

'Isn't that fish?'

'Gourmet fish! Dessert! Oh *can* you smell it! Ooh-lah-lah!'

Wilson, moving deliberately, divested himself of the black raincoat and, holding it wide, like a net, poised behind the sandwich. The trap was set.

Fiston, fresh in his role of provider and caretaker, rose to a sitting position. He could sense Wilson readily enough. Not even the powerful odour of the sardines could mask that musty smell. Having been raised as a domesticated creature, human emanations were familiar and did not particularly bother him. Fiston began to walk slowly, tail twitching, in the direction of the alluring scent, pausing only to mark the territory in the vicinity.

'Miaaaouuwww,' said Fiston tentatively, to the curious apparition squatting by the sandwich.

'Zat's a coot kitty,' whispered Wilson, hardly moving his lips. A sudden move now would wreck everything. To his delight and astonishment Fiston approached within two feet and sniffed delicately the offering with distended nostrils. He paused, looked at Wilson, sniffed again, and then gave the sandwich a tentative look. Then, even more remarkable, he ambled over to the thunderstruck Wilson and rubbed the side of his face on Wilson's bony knee. For an instant Wilson was nonplussed. The cat was so disarmingly confident and trusting. This was obviously not a feral cat.

In that second Willy came to his senses. In a flash he flung the coat over Fiston, bundling the startled creature into a tight, untidy ball. Fiston responded with a bewildered and then frantic, 'Miaaoouwww!!' In a split second, his plaintive voice changed into a muffled, furious growl as he struggled to free himself. The white cat froze in her tracks. Wilson, beside himself with elation and relief, tightened the belt of the raincoat around the bundle and the terrified cat. Fiston's muffled screeching and clawing at the cloth were to no avail, the raincoat had him helpless. He could hardly breathe and lapsed into petrified silence punctuated by an occasional, deep, throaty growl.

Wilson, his great prize secure, tottered back to his parked car, opened the boot, wound a piece of rope around the raincoat for good measure, and slammed the boot shut. Thirty minutes later he was back in his laboratory.

Fiston came to his senses in a wooden cage with a window of steel bars set in one side. Peering at him was Willy Wilson, the cat mortician, rubbing his hands, and studying him with a practised eye. Wilson realized he had a problem. His clients usually arrived in a defunct state. He'd never actually been required to euthanize a subject. How to do it? Obviously there had to be no sign of injury. What to do? He knew little about anaesthetics. Poison . . . but what sort?

Carol sprinted as fast as her legs would allow. Breathless, she paused at the end of the lane and looked back. Fiston had not followed. She began, very cautiously, to retrace her steps. She passed by the rear of *Alphen House*. The yard was empty. She walked on. Soon she came across the discarded sardine sandwich. After a cursory inspection she ignored what had been a delicious treat and raised her head. Where was her hero? She let out a series of plaintive calls. There was no answer. Her spirits sinking, she walked on. There was no hope, she was alone again. Then, rounding a corner she came face to face with a well fed, long haired Persian tom clearly in his prime.

'Hi babe,' purred the Persian, calm and confident, 'what's up?'

'I'm looking for a friend.'

'Will I do?' Despite her distress Carol could not help noticing he was gorgeous and exuded that special, not-so-subtle aroma of an intact male cat.

'I'm serious. My best friend, a Russian Blue, Fiston, has disappeared. I . . . I suspect foul play. He's been catnapped!'

'Fiston? What sort of name's that? Is he a poofder?'

Carol began to weep and turned away. The Persian, embarrassed, relented.

'Look, I was joking. My name's Adrian, by the way. Is, er, there anything I can do to help?'

Carol stopped and walked slowly back,

'Have you seen anybody, or anything, suspicious in this lane?'

'Babe, everything in this lane is suspicious. This is where we find, er, rubby-dubs, pimps, thieves and, if you'll pardon the expression, red-hot queens. This is where fish head dealers hang around. This is,' he looked her over with a practised eye, 'no place for a lady of class.'

'Have you seen a seedy looking human drive off in a black van with gold lettering?'

'As a matter of fact I have. I was heading south, following my nose to some fishy object, when a black van nearly ran over me.'

Carol could not hide her excitement.

'Where . . . I suppose it's no use asking . . . did it go?'

'You're in luck,' said the Persian, 'I happen to know that outfit. Me and my friends give it a wide berth. It's usually parked out on the main street. We've, even for us, seen strange sights coming and going. Bodies . . . you know. Carried in and out all the time.'

'What strange sights? What bodies?' A chill hand clutched Carol's heart.

'Humans walk in with sacks, or suitcases, and later leave with an animal. An animal, like us, only it doesn't move.'

'Doesn't move?'

'Deaded. Stuffed. Some nutty humans keep a pet, stuffed, in their homes.'

'How horrible. Can you, will you, take me there?'

The tom walked slowly around Carol, examining her state of health in minute detail. She showed promise.

'I suppose I could. But there's a risk . . . and a price.'

'Anything,' replied Carol, without thinking. The tom was turning out to be another hero. And, he was attractive.

On the main street, rows of parked cars stretched for blocks. Halfway down the street the two cats, walking in single file came across *the* van with the faded gold lettering on its sides.

'Wait here,' ordered the Persian, and leaped lightly onto the sill of the window opposite the van and facing the street. The accumulation of years of dirt obscured the glass and he could see very little.

'We'll have to go round the back.'

No sooner had they found their way around the back alley, when Carol was shocked to find that Adrian seemed to have other things on his mind. He began to nuzzle her and to make bloodcurdling noises. It soon dawned on her – her own desires were stirring – what Adrian was after. Backing off rapidly she snapped, 'No. Not now! Perhaps later. This is *not* the place. First things first. We must find Fiston!'

'Oh, so that's it. Using me to save your lover. I'm not good enough?'

'Come on. It's not like that. Fiston's a great cat, but he's not like you. We are friends, just great *friends*. I love him, but differently. I must find him. Later,' she shrugged. 'Who knows? BUT NOT NOW.'

Adrian sat and gazed at beautiful Carol. Finally, making up his mind, he agreed and scrambled onto a tin shed, and leaped gracefully several feet to land precariously on a high window sill.

'I can see inside,' he called down, 'it's a sort of mad professor's workshop. Wait . . ., there's a box in the corner with bars. Yes! I see him. A cat. A Russian Blue did you say?'

'Yes,' Carol could not contain her excitement. 'Is he all right?'

'Well, he's moving. Pacing back and forth.'

'Oh, thank heaven,' breathed Carol, 'thank you . . . thank you. Oh, what a relief.'

Adrian, paused, judged his distance, and with two, neatly timed leaps came down to ground level. He was rather pleased with himself. Carol rewarded him with a grateful lick.

Chapter 8

Oscar to the Rescue

'What on earth do we do now?' Carol, beside herself with excitement and anxiety, followed Adrian down the alley, retracing their steps. Before Adrian could come up with an intelligent reply she spoke again, 'What I *should* do is to head back to his human home and fetch human help. Do you think . . . would you . . . could you come along, Adrian?'

'This Fiston guy . . . he means a lot to you?'

'Yes, he does. He made me feel there was more to me than just another pretty fur coat. For once I wasn't simply a sex object. We were, are, very close, really close. You do understand?'

'Not exactly,' said Adrian, whose hormones were spinning frantically, 'but if you want me to, I'll help.' He was rewarded with a long, searching look. Carol was racked with similarly disturbing, conflicting emotions.

'You will?'

Adrian hesitated. What have I to lose? he thought, she's gorgeous. Maybe when all this settles . . . when her so-called friend's safe? His romantic imagination began to soar.

'Okay,' he said, at last, 'let's move, I'm getting hungry. Is it far, his human home?'

Like every cat in the world, Carol held imprinted in her

brain, the exact route to Fiston's house, or at least to a place within a stone's throw from it, where first they'd met. Precisely how they would organize help had not yet been worked out. She was acutely aware that time was not on their side.

Late that evening two travel worn cats arrived at the fence that ran along the back of Fiston's owner's property. Tracing Fiston's scent from the bush where she'd accosted him had been straightforward enough.

'I don't know about you,' complained Adrian, 'but if I don't eat soon I'll be no use.'

Carol looked around. Fortunately, several yellow plastic garbage bags had been carelessly deposited on the lids of largely empty garbage cans. The twins were not fussy about how they disposed of garbage. As far as they were concerned garbage simply melted away mysteriously. It certainly had nothing to do with them. It was an unfair, onerous task forced on them by ungrateful parents. Whoever'd been on garbage duty had simply dumped over-filled bags carelessly, onto instead of into a small garbage enclosure built in the fence. In this instance their efforts, or lack of them, were much appreciated. Soon Carol and Adrian were feasting on a variety of leftovers and discarded dishes.

Halfway through their refreshing meal a deafening bark penetrated the wooden fence like an exploding shell sending Carol and Adrian several feet into the air.

'Oh my God, it must be Oscar,' gulped Carol, when she regained her breath, 'That's him all right. I know about him. Fiston told me about him. Don't worry he's safe . . . on the other side of that fence.'

'So you say,' growled Adrian, ears flattened along his skull, fur erect. 'Doesn't sound exactly welcoming.'

'He doesn't know us. I'll try to reason with him.'

'Good luck!'

Oscar, incensed now, continued to bark with increasing ferocity and intensity. Cats were natural enemies and here, of all the cheeky nerve, they were poaching in his territory!

'Oscar,' called Carol. But Oscar's deafening hullabaloo drowned her efforts. '*Oscar!*' she screeched between barks. Oscar paused, puzzled. Generally he'd not deigned to understand or speak cat language, but he recognized his name. It was her pleading tone which baffled him more than anything else.

'Oscar,' called Carol, more softly. Oscar lurched forward, eyes bulging, head angled, ears erect, as he approached the chain link fence.

'What do you want?' he growled, in a semi-bark.

'I'm a friend of Fiston's . . . no wait,' Carol added hastily as Oscar took a deep, preparatory breath, 'Fiston's in deadly danger.' She spoke very slowly and clearly, 'He needs your help.'

The idea of Fiston, who generally disdained Oscar's existence, needing his help was a novel concept. Oscar closed his jaws and waited for an explanation.

'*He's been abducted,*' Carol continued to speak slowly and distinctly, 'and will probably be killed . . . very soon, unless he's rescued. Please . . . will you help?' Oscar approached closer to the fence and peered suspiciously through it in case it was some trick of the St Bernard thugs. But he saw only two small outlines.

'And who did you say you were?' he barked.

An idea occurred to Carol, 'I met Fiston a few days ago, after he left home. After he split . . . to leave the house to yourself . . . for you, Oscar.'

'For me? He did that? I find that hard to believe,' growled Oscar, incredulously.

'He thought you'd be happier without him around. Look, Oscar can you put aside your animosity? If we succeed in rescuing him, you'll be a hero. Fiston, the humans, and me, will forever be in your debt. You could get a medal from the Governor General. The Order of Canada for bravery. You could wear it on your collar. And think of it you two have known each other for years. Please . . . we must help. *I* can't speak to your humans.'

'Izzat so,' Oscar said, sardonically, still not sure this was not some sort of elaborate joke, 'well I can't either.' Sounds grand . . . medals on my collar . . . hmmm, he pondered, on the other hand I don't have any fond feelings for that self-satisfied cat. Yet, when he's away I feel an emptiness. Weird.

As if reading his mind Carol spoke,

'Sure you do. You miss him don't you? Well, here's your chance to rise above ordinary canine feelings. You could show him . . . what you really are made of . . . who's the better, er, person.' Oscar pondered this extraordinary notion.

'What can I do, assuming I agreed?'

'We'll think of something. First you must agree.'

'All right,' grumbled Oscar, uncertainly.

'Let's see now . . . what about your humans? They take you for walks don't they? You could drag them, or lead them, to the place they're holding Fiston. We'll show you the way.'

'*I* don't arrange walks. They do. But, I suppose I could try.' Oscar was beginning to soften. 'No, it wouldn't work. They *always* go the same old way.'

'Try begging. Think of feeding time. Don't you watch them eat? Stare at them at table. Use your brains. You must! Time is too short. Put on an act. Bring them your leash. I've heard of dogs doing just that. It seems to work, at least on TV.'

'My leash? Hmmmm . . . not a bad idea. I'll think it over.'

'No, please . . . do it NOW. You must act, before it's too late. Fiston may be a stuffed statue in the very near future.' Oscar thought this idea seemed to have merit.

'Please, please, Oscar, we'll all be eternally grateful. And so will Fiston. And the humans will never be able to thank you enough. It *is* a matter of life and death.'

'How will they know what to do? Anyway, I've got to go now. I'll see what can be done. It's too late for a walk. You can sleep by those cans,' he added magnanimously.

The next morning, a Sunday, Oscar rose at dawn to the usual chorus of screeching magpies. Largely to thwart their cunning habits with his breakfast, he finished the remains of the meal in his bowl, and only then pursued the magpies theatrically. All the while he was thinking. What to do? Last night's conversation seemed quite unreal in the light of day. Did it happen? Anyway, here goes, he thought, and strolled over to mount the stairs leading to the French windows in the breakfast room. It was too early. The room was empty. He curled up to nap and wait. An hour passed. Oscar woke to the sound of dishes clattering in the breakfast room. He rushed off to retrieve his leash draped over the temperature gauge projecting by the French windows. On the way back, to announce his presence, he stopped to bark at imaginary magpies. When he reached the French windows he sat, leash in his mouth, staring fixedly through the glass.

'I say,' said Edward, the under leader of the pack, looking up from the newspaper propped over his cereal, 'it's Oscar. And I do believe, for the first time since I've known him, he's giving us a sign! Amazing! I can't resist this. The old boy wants to go walkabout.'

The twin girls, their faces swollen from lack of sleep and worry – Fiston had been missing for four days – hardly looked up.

'Come on you two zombies, cheer up! Get dressed and take him for a walk.'

'We've homework to do and I'm waiting for a phone call and I've got to do my nails. Beside it's her turn (indicating her twin) to take the garbage out, and I'm expecting a phone call.'

'You've said that twice. Look you two,' thundered the alpha female of the pack, 'get dressed now and see to it for once. Stop your whining. *Do it now!* Oscar needs attention. Anyway, while you're out you'd discover something novel . . . for you . . . fresh air, heard of that? And maybe, a clue about Fiston's whereabouts. He could have moved in next door. You never clean out his litter box. By the way, I hear there's a new boy on the block.'

'Who cares about men. They're all the same. They're all slimes.'

'Except Peter, in England,' protested the older twin. 'Anyway it's too late. Fiston's probably been killed by a car, or something worse.'

'Look here,' said the lady leader, trying to reason with her chronically recalcitrant offspring, 'It's for your own good. Do as your father says for once, or no TV or phone . . . all day!' That threat took root.

The younger twin let off her customary steam engine sigh and, flouncing out, shouted over her retreating shoulder, 'Okay, okay, okay . . . *I will*. Don't nag.'

'Both of you. Out!'

Their father suppressed a grin.

Thirty minutes later, dressed to the nines – top heavy with

make-up in case there were any new males about – cursing dreadfully enough for drunken sailors, the twins fastened the leash to Oscar's collar and took off. Oscar began immediately to choke on his collar as he struggled ahead dragging them on the long leash. His eyes were focused on two furry tails well ahead. He strained and coughed convincingly as he literally towed the reluctant humans behind him. Now and then, in order to keep up a pretence of a normal walkies, he paused to deposit a single drop of urine on a blade of grass. In this way, the small expedition, an asphyxiating dog leading bellyaching girls, preceded by two distant cats, made its way slowly to the main drag in the town.

Half an hour later they rounded the first corner in the main street and walked on past closed shops for several blocks until they came to a major crossroads. A short distance ahead Oscar spotted the pathfinders on the roof of a black, small van with faded gold lettering on its sides. Both cats sat with their noses pointing resolutely at a door in the building opposite the van. In short order Oscar and his trailing crew of two drew abreast a dimly illuminated filthy shop window. Oscar looked up at the cats, stopped, and squatted firmly on his haunches. He refused to budge. The girls, glad for a breather and an opportunity to repair their multi-layered make-up, stepped up to the grimy glass and studied their reflections minutely. As they did so they chanced to looked past the dirt encrusted surface of the glass into the interior of the building. Oscar and company watched and waited with bated breath.

For a few seconds the girls smeared additional layers of lipstick on their mouths. After a moment or two something moving inside caught their attention. Beyond their reflections they made out a motley collection of stuffed owls, coyotes, and a mangy cat or two. The whole place was heavily encrusted with cobwebs. It was spooky. The business, whatever it was, seemed slack or non-existent. In the background Carol and Adrian quivered with excitement.

Just then the bizarre figure of Willy Wilson, clad in a red rubber apron and heavy black leather gloves staggered down the stairs bearing a wooden box with iron bars on one side. In his left hand he held a glass flask with a rubber stopper. By now the twins, their made up images and Oscar forgotten, looked on, fascinated. What was going on? What was that awful man up to? It seemed *really* gruesome. In fact they decided, glancing at each other, that the scene inside was as terrifying as any horror movie.

They continued to watch in growing, fascinated consternation. Willy Wilson staggered over to a bench and unstoppered the flask. He pulled a ghastly face and staggered back as pungent vapours enveloped his proboscis. Holding the open flask in his left hand, he turned and raised the lid of the box with the other hand. What happened next was extraordinary.

Fiston, who'd been lying inert and apparently stunned on the floor of the box, let out a piercing screech that penetrated the plate glass window as if it was paper. Like a flash he squirted out of the opening in the box and, in one bound, landed on the highest object he could see, the top of a hat rack. The twins couldn't believe their eyes and stood horror struck, mouths slack and open.

Fiston's leap brought him to rest by a frayed, stuffed owl perched on the free standing rack. But his momentum caused him to teeter back and forth. For a second he struggled to regain his balance, but to no avail. In slow motion, but gathering speed rapidly, the hat rack, Fiston, and the stuffed owl descended and crashed on the stupefied taxidermist. Willy Wilson, née Wilhelmstein, was knocked stone cold. Colourless liquid from the bottle spilled out over his red rubber apron and seeped onto his collar.

At this point the dumbfounded twins, having finally grasped that their long lost baby was in mortal danger, came to life and started shrieking in unison as only distressed teenaged girls can.

Windows began to open. Heads popped out.

'What's that racket? What's going on?'

The older twin found her voice.

'It's our cat, Fiston!' she shrieked, 'he's *inside*. Someone's trying to poison him . . . HELP! HELP!'

An elderly, half drunk, retired dentist in an apartment opposite tried to dial 911. After three attempts he succeeded. Within minutes the wail of a police siren could be heard in the far distance.

Carol and Adrian, the successful pathfinders, purred with delicious happiness and satisfaction. It was all too marvellous! Oscar watched all this in amazement. The noise was tremendously stimulating! He rediscovered his voice and joined the chorus with enthusiastic thunderous, ecstatic barks. A small crowd gathered. The fire department was the first to arrive. Two firemen broke down the front door releasing a stench of chloroform and dead meat. Inside they found a scene from a Dickens novel. The taxidermist, dragged out feet first, was left lying in the fresh air, coughing and choking. No one volunteered to give him the kiss of life. Despite the lack of medical attention, slowly he regained his senses. He began to roll about, still spluttering vigorously. Soon he was breathing normally.

When he'd repossessed control of his lungs and his wits Willy Wilson sat up, stared around, totally bemused by the enormous activity. What had happened? How did he get there? His last memory was of a Russian Blue cat leaping from the box. Had he been dreaming? Was it the chloroform? Oh, my God, he thought, bleakly, what about Mrs Beck's cat?

As soon as the heavy vapours of chloroform were dispelled from the room the overwrought twins rushed in, moistened handkerchiefs tied dramatically around their noses, to rescue their baby. They discovered Fiston sheltering behind a pile of boxes. He trembled with terror and clung to them and sank his claws into their clothed arms. The delighted twins bore the pain without protest. Their darling was safe!

Outside, uncharacteristically, Oscar had stopped barking and sat quietly on his haunches, his leash dangling unattended. No one paid him any attention. Carol and Adrian sidled up.

'Oscar,' purred Carol, leaning against Adrian, '*you* did it. *You* are the hero. No one else in the whole wide world could've done it. But you did. We'll never think of dogs in the same way again. I hope Fiston will realize he owes you his life.'

Oscar raised a floppy ear, tilted his head, and looked directly at the snow white cat and her nervous Persian companion and, for once, refrained from barking. There was no need. He had proved himself.

Epilogue

The atmosphere in the court room on this final day of Fiston's trial was tense and unsettled. The jury had been out fourteen hours. The judge, ostensibly waiting in his chambers, had given up and was out hunting voles with cronies in a nearby field. He was equipped with the latest feline equivalent of a cellular phone. A specially trained field mouse waited in a cage in the judge's chambers to be released as soon as the jury signalled a decision imminent. His Lordship was about to tee off for the ninth vole, when a squeak from the field mouse interrupted. He turned and sniffed the air. It was the special mouse. The jury was about to return.

'Drat that cat,' cursed the judge. He was especially peeved because up to that point his score was notably low, partly the result of creative mathematics which he hoped had been unobserved.

'I'm afraid it's back to the grindstone. The jury's returning. One certainly earns one's money in this business.'

Less than thirty minutes later the solemn clerk intoned, 'All rise.'

His lordship stalked in. He gave every impression of having spent hours pouring over tomes overflowing with legal precedents and grey areas. In a few minutes the door to the jury room opened and an assortment of bleary eyed cats filed into the court.

'Stand and face the jury,' ordered the clerk of the court to Fiston. The moment of truth is here! Gold help me, thought Fiston.

'Toms and Queens of the jury have you reached a verdict?'

'We have,' replied the alpha cat-foreman.

'And is it the verdict of you all?'

The foreman paused, took a deep breath and said,

'It is. We, the jury, find the defendant not guilty.'

An audible gasp rose from the packed room. The judge scowled. What a waste of his time. No bloody death sentence. Oh, well, he thought, at least this won't take long. Got no choice but to let the blighter off. Might impress my new wife if I make a show of mercy by agreeing and congratulating that jury. His countenance brightened. Into his mind flashed the headlines of the morning paper,

'Judge endorses Jury's mercy recommendation to fellow cat.'

All that power . . . all that veneration . . . was his! Life, after all, was sweet. Yes, he thought, after all's said and done, my power is immense. For a full minute he sat staring at the wall at the rear of the court, lost in thought.

'Fiston, you have heard the verdict of the court,' intoned his Lordship, automatically. 'You have been found not guilty by a jury of your peers. I agree. You are free to go.'

The applause was deafening.

'Order, order,' called the clerk, without enthusiasm.

Fiston, a hint of moisture glistening in his eyes, looked around for Carol. But she was not in court. Ah, he thought, sadly, she needs someone else, younger. A faster, newer, and more able model. What can I offer one so young and so fertile? She's probably embarrassed by my elderly presence.

A totally novel thought intruded. What about Oscar? Where was his saviour? Probably not allowed into a cat court. He'd start a new life . . . a new friendship. The idea was not comfortable, but not displeasing. The cold war was over. In this righteous state of mind he left the witness box and walked over to thank his counsel and, without a backward glance, walked out into the street and headed for home. There were worse fates than living a pampered life with twin humans and a dog, for protectors. They owe me something. They saved my life.

Outside, across the street, a snow white queen sat and watched as Fiston walked steadily homeward. She sighed, looked down, and shook her head, her eyes brimming with tears. Adrian, tactfully, affected not to see. After a few moments he strolled nonchalantly off in the opposite direction. Carol watched until Fiston was well out of sight, and then turned slowly to follow Adrian and a new life.